THE
REFLECTED SELF

BY KELVIN RICHARDS

Dedicated to my wife, Holly
for both believing in me,
and putting up with me.

Prologue

A single window atop a mortared stone wall radiates with sunlight through its thin pane of glass. Timber beams engulf the room situated below, whilst the spotlight of midday etches itself into the centre of exposed wooden floorboards. Once a bustling building of local necessity, this converted sixteenth-century mill house now sits with a bleak abundance of life, whilst once-loved trinkets reside on worn furniture with an eerie stillness, untouched for decades and now blanketed with cotton dust sheets.

Gently descending, glimmering particles of dust offer the only sign that time still passes here.

The deathly silence is soon disturbed however, when distant footsteps draw ever closer. The house sits attentively until a key is inserted into its rustic doorway, the lock cracking like old bones whilst its hinges wail with relief as the door creaks open, providing the house with its first breath after years of solitude. Daylight forces itself into this once darkened space, as two new residents prepare to enter the dormant dwelling.

Dion's boots pound heavily into the wooden floorboards as they screech to support his stocky six-foot, one-hundred and ninety-six pound frame. The removal of his cap reveals a clean shaven face and short dark hair that is now starting to fade as he edges closer to forty than thirty, but the spring in his step and Sinatra blue eyes tell a much younger tale. In his hands rests a heavy cardboard box, filled just enough to ensure the top panels can't rest comfortably closed. He abruptly hauls the box onto the side cabinet as a cloud of dust erupts from beneath, followed immediately by his spluttering.

At almost half his age, but twice as fashionable, follows his sister, Nia. A short, petit girl with dark brown hair and juxtaposing bright blue eyes. Also carrying a heavy cardboard box, she wrestles her way beside Dion as he instinctively takes the box from her.

"I had it!" she protests.

Dion offers an apologetic smile then, not learning from his first dust cloud, hauls the second box onto the cabinet - caking them both. After a moment of settlement, the two brush themselves down and gaze with unfamiliarity at their new surroundings. Somber oak consumes every inch of the hallway and continues to rise up the meandering staircase as fractures of windows provide little incandescence to this desolate nebulous.

"It's…" Nia mutters.

Dion shoots her a look and with silent acknowledgement she changes tack.

"I was going to say it's really nice!" she proclaims with mock astonishment.

Dion nods contritely and they both reset to gaze upon the emptiness of the hallway before them.

"Got a great personality I'm sure." She concludes with a smirk.

Much to his dismay, Dion has always found his younger sibling's dry wit amusing and although desperately trying to suppress a smile, it eventually paints itself onto the corner of his mouth. Noticing the slight curvature, Nia offers an affirmative nod at her achievement, then walks down the hallway to investigate their new home. Dion turns and manages to close the front door on his third attempt, then wiping the remainder of dust from his arms, something, or someone, catches his eye. He glances up and his suspicions are confirmed.

A woman is now stood at the entrance to the long dark hallway, her pale white eyes burning into his. He stands motionless, as does the world around him. Although dressed in what would be considered normal attire, her flowing dark hair covers the features of a looming pale face, and he can see there is no colour to her eyes, just two deeply set pearlescent spheres.

The creak of a floorboard averts his attention as Nia returns but his attempts to protect her go in vain as he remains motionless with paralysing fear - trying to scream but finding his cries trapped as thoughts. To his surprise, Nia strides directly past the woman without any hesitation, their faces mere inches apart. She flings open one of the cardboard box panels and begins to rummage inside. Hearing his calls echo within the walls of his own mind, Dion pauses as the situation takes a drastic turn.

The woman is no longer stood still, her head is moving, slowly panning across the hallway until coming to a sudden halt.

Nia is now the target of her gaze.

Trying desperately to fight the feeling of paralysis, Dion can only watch as the woman begins walking towards Nia. One foot silently creeping in-front of the other, and now gaining momentum. Nia's search continues, blissfully unaware of the impending danger as the woman's hand begins to outstretch towards her.

With every fibre ignoring his instruction, Dion's body remains useless in a fugue-like state until Nia finally removes a book from the box and with a sigh of relief, turns to leave the room - her hair brushing past the woman's

reachi
an aw

St

T
tranc

T
her
dov
wit

Th

A large dust sheet
drawers beneath
the white c
Nia's be
both

glides from the wooden antique chest of ..., as Dion and Nia continue to remove all of ...tton sheets covering items of furniture within ...droom. A grey haze now clouds the room and they ...remain motionless until it clears, unearthing the dreary ...oom within, encapsulated in deep brown oak - wooden beams, walls and ceiling - with only a small window allowing a streak of daylight to enter, not large enough for Nia's petit frame to escape, should she need to.

Whilst starting to familiarise with her new surroundings, Nia comes to accept the fact that this will be a more minimalistic approach than she's accustomed to, but at least it provides her with a writing desk, wardrobe, and bed. The essentials none the less.

"I can work with this." Nia agrees with herself.

"You sure?"

Nia takes another glance and offers an uncertain nod when she notices a fallen picture frame laid atop the writing desk. Never one to leave things convoluted, she takes a closer look - the frailty of its wooden border feeling as though it will break in her hands should she squeeze too tight, and upon turning it over, the picture inside reveals itself to be the portrait of a young Victorian woman. The years of sun-damage are prevalent and a burned line has etched itself across the woman's eyes.

Nia glances the picture in her brother's direction and asks, "Who's this?"

Dion briefly glimpses then very matter-of-factly explains, "Doris."

Nia looks back at the picture. She has never heard of a Doris in the family and questions further, "Doris?"

Dion begins to laugh at her naivety and Nia reciprocates in amusement at his attempted joke.

He continues, "I don't know, it must be a great, great someone we're related to?" whilst walking towards Nia and taking a hold of the frame.

He looks deep into the picture - her likeness to the woman he saw in the hallway causes immediate discomfort. Especially those burned out eyes. Once again he is transfixed on her, unable to look away. Having tried to forget the encounter (presuming it was just fatigue from travelling, or perhaps an 'undigested bit of beef') it strikes him as implausible to be pure coincidence that her picture now finds itself in his trembling hands.

Seeing his vacant expression, Nia asks, "Dion?"

As though coming up for air he gasps, "Yes?"

Taking a beat for dramatic emphasis, Nia continues, "Shall I leave you and the picture alone for a while?"

He chuckles, suddenly ignoring all presumptive notions about the picture and confidently returns the frame before continuing to unbox items.

Nia takes a hold and studies the picture in more detail. She can't help but try to imagine who this woman could be, how she came to be here in this picture, and equally (and more selfishly) what the two of them now living here would mean to her own story. Grasping the picture, Nia walks over to the bed and takes a seat, with yet another puff of dust emitting from the depths of antiquities. Whilst looking at all of the surrounding oak beams and hearing the ambient roar of water gushing beneath the old mill, she begins to articulate her thoughts, "There must be so much history here," then hesitates before concluding, "strange to think that we're now a part of it."

Dion hears the slight choke in her voice and turns to find Nia's face dropping with hopelessness.

"Hey, there's like 3 other rooms if you don't like this one?" he offers in a panicked response.

Nia shakes her head, looking to the ground, "No it's fine. It's not the room."

Dion's chest implodes at the thought of Nia being upset. He's always had murmurings in the depths of his conscience that everything he's doing is not enough, but this confirms it, and he soon finds himself slumping beside her. She slowly rests her head against his shoulder and he naturally lowers his cheek atop her forehead as they sit in contemplative silence. Dion can feel her thoughts flying through his own mind - the worry, the doubt, the sadness - although, he cannot be certain whether it is simply a projection of his own concerns, but quickly ignores the inference.

"I promise I'll make this work," he claims with confidence, trying to comfort her, and it seems to work as she responds from the depths of his shoulder.

"I know," Nia rises from her position and continues, "because if you don't..."

She clenches her right hand into a fist then punches it into her open left hand with a thud, mocking the action of a bully. A relieved smile breaks on Dion's face and he can't help but throw his arm around her whilst messing her hair with the other.

The kitchen sits with an aura of calmness, disturbed only by the intermittent tapping of droplets falling rhythmically from its leaking brass faucet - and by the commotion caused by Dion's fumbling as he carries eight overfilled shopping bags, four in each hand. Eventually reaching the fridge, he lowers them to the ground then studies the white indented pressure marks striped across his hands with a grimace.

He soon begins removing items from the bags and places them onto the side cabinet, proudly revealing a healthy display of eggs, fruits, vegetables and bagels. Dion rarely eats like this, in-fact, he can't even remember the last time he ate an apple, but without the faintest idea on how to take care of an adolescent (let alone himself for that matter) Dion finds he is continually selecting actions based on what he imagines wider society would deem as 'correct' - and surely this type of dietary choice is better than his usual meals, right? Plus, he knows that taking better care of himself is imperative now, to ensure he hangs around for as long as possible for Nia's sake - so positives on all fronts.

From the depths of the house he hears Nia calling, "Dion?"

The smile slowly spreading across his face reveals he has no intention of answering, merely trying to infuriate his younger sibling. It soon works.

"Dion!?" Nia calls even louder, her voice echoing throughout the house.

He continues to unpack whilst listening to the stomping of wooden floorboards from the level below him until Nia eventually appears. Reciprocating her brother's antics, she runs over to the shopping bags and purposefully positions herself between Dion and the fridge.

"What you get? What you get? You making pancakes?" she asks playfully.

With great difficulty, Dion manages to continue unpacking the bags of shopping until Nia's investigation abruptly stops. It's an array of healthy food.

"Oh," her face fills with dismay.

Dion's smile appears once again, as though preempting the response, whilst Nia stares blankly.

He states, "Your blood pressure will thank me when you're older."

"Living with you is going to give me higher blood pressure than any food!" she retorts.

The joke catches him unaware and he is unable to hide his laughter. Nia gushes with pride then looks down at her dietary options, eventually deciding upon the most sugary item available and snatches a shining red apple. Taking one large gleeful bite, she turns to Dion with a mouthful and splutters the words "Hmm forbidden fruit. I'm going to take a walk."

"Where?" Dion replies instinctively.

Nia tilts her head and gives a very nonchalant glare. Although overstepping his boundaries, Dion remains true to his initial concern.

"Just be careful."

Nia is about to leave when the burning desire to say something overcomes her.

"If it's just going to be the two of us, then I can't be your only hobby."

Although trying to mask the truth with humour, they both know this is something Dion is guilty of.

Whether through selfishness or simply the act of growing up, the slight age gap between the siblings meant that Dion was ready to fly the nest when Nia was still a young girl, and he flew the moment his wings allowed. But as time passed, so did their relationship, and the visits home began to dwindle - turning from weekly to fortnightly, monthly to annually, until eventually he was just absent from her life entirely. It was not something Dion dwelled on overly, just something that came with age and 'finding one's self' - but with everything that has since happened, it's all he can think about. Acknowledging that he had nothing to do with Nia growing into this confident young woman, Dion now desperately wants to rectify his mistakes. Without any previous experience on the matter of parenting, Dion finds himself trying to fulfil the role of disciplinarian, when in actual fact, it's far too late for that now, and what she really needs is her big brother. It's just something he's finding difficult to shake.

Nia takes another bite of the apple then is about to leave when Dion decides to have the last word and correct his approach, "I had a Snickers on the way back." He grins.

Nia stops in the doorway, completely lost for words and can't hide the shock on her face as she turns to confront him. Using the universal sign for 'I'm watching you', Nia points two fingers towards her eyes and then at Dion's, slowly walking backwards out of the door, to great effect.

Dion stands before the window and watches as his little sister wanders through the large grounds surrounding the house. He smiles. She still walks the same, he thinks to himself - instantly those painful thoughts come flooding back. After such a long time apart, being thrown back together again in such awful circumstances hasn't been easy on either of them, but the overwhelming need to care for her is almost unbearable at times. He begins to recite the events of that fateful night, when the floorboard directly above him creaks.

Pausing momentarily to look up, he hears the creak once again, one or two steps ahead of the last.

Holding his breath, Dion waits for another sound, but the atmosphere is merely filled with silence. He exhales with relief and continues unpacking when even louder footsteps run across the entire length of the room above. Thud, thud, thud.

He flinches and drops some of the shopping onto the floor with a loud crash, the remaining apples rolling beneath the cabinet. His pounding heart is the only sound to be heard whilst trying to listen again. Regaining composure, he heads towards the kitchen door and slowly peers around the corner into the hallway. Empty.

Standing deathly still, the silence grows louder. Dion takes a single step forward and pauses, listening to the silence once again, then proceeds to creep to the bottom of the winding staircase where he comes to an abrupt halt. Having familiarised himself with the house somewhat, he knows these old rickety stairs are going to scream with each step, and so he dismisses his initial tactical approach, stands tall, and begins to confidently climb the staircase. Albeit, terrified.

Holding onto the bannister, he feels the beads of sweat leaving a trail behind as he climbs each step. Reaching the top of the staircase reveals the vast, empty room where only a chair and side table reside. The noise has stopped, but his heart has not and he stands motionless whilst scanning the room. It's completely empty except for the single picture frame now sat on the side table, inviting him, and he cautiously begins walking towards it. The closer he gets the more clearly he can see it's the same picture from Nia's bedroom. But what is it doing here?

Uncontrollably, his hand reaches and takes a hold of the frame. There she sits, that same woman with the dark hair and burned out eyes once again haunting him.

"Dion!" the call of his name causes such alarm that he instantly drops the picture frame onto the floor as the glass shatters into pieces at his feet. He turns to find Nia gleefully looking at him from across the room and, as relieved as he may feel, an old-fashioned look begins to mould itself onto his face.

"Is this because of the Snickers?" he pleads whilst holding his chest.

"Hey, you bring me to Norman Bates' house, what else am I supposed to do in my spare time?" she says with a titter.

The rapturous sound of her laughter reminds Dion of the times their family would all sit and watch the comedy show 'Friends' together, whilst her giggling would paint itself colourfully throughout the house. But as the memory fades, sadness ensues. It's now an unfamiliar sound.

And in that moment he decides, if it means taking a few cat years off his life to make her happy, then he can be that outlet. Giving a wry smile (and just as Nia begins to think he's going to admit defeat) Dion holds two fists up and knocks them together twice with dramatic emphasis, imitating an old joke from their once beloved TV show. Dion holds a moment longer to see her reaction, but those nights gathered around the TV are clearly not shared memories as she offers a mere smile - a devastating blow.

"Well I was going to help tidy that up, but now you're on your own!" she laughs then heads back downstairs, true to her word.

Once she has disappeared out of sight, panic erupts and Dion collapses onto one knee beside the picture, trying to catch his breath whilst the woman blindly stares at him through shattered glass. He can't help but think, this may not be last time he will have to endure this woman's torturous stare.

2

A peppering of cardboard boxes occupy the floor in Dion's bedroom - a small room with a single bed, writing desk and window positioned at waist height (well, knee height for someone of Dion's stature) amongst rustic wooden panelling covering every wall. Standing amongst the sea of boxes with hands on hips, he hasn't the faintest idea of where to begin or even what to do, which then progresses to the realisation that this isn't necessarily in reference to the boxes.

What *are* we going to do? He thinks to himself. After the fire, all he knew was that he needed to take Nia far away and protect her. The plan had no further steps, but he knew as long as she was with him, he could keep her safe.

They had now fulfilled 'Step One' of his masterplan rather adequately, and the fact that 'Step Two' hadn't spawned yet didn't phase him. They were here, together.

He finds the procrastinating thought leading his mind down a path he doesn't want to explore yet, and so he attempts to distract himself by unpacking the box closest to him, ripping off the brown tape and flinging open the panels.

His idea of distraction has gone awry. Whether it is serendipitous or mere coincidence he cannot fathom right now, but at the very top of the box lay a bundle of items tightly concealed in bubble wrap, yet he knows exactly what awaits him beneath that layer of protection. They are the very items that will force him to face the truth of their residency here, and he knows now is the time to endure it. Dion closes the panels and takes the box under his arm.

Upon entering the living room, Dion searches for the best location to host these items. The room features a large open-plan design with a small table, chairs, sofas and cabinets sporadically placed throughout. He begins to wander, ducking beneath the low-hanging oak beams floating every three meters, and stands in the centre of the room perusing his options. Eventually he decides the empty bookcase in the far corner is best suited with its prominent position beside the window that floods the room with daylight, and strides ahead - the box still securely beneath his arm.

Now standing before the bookcase, he pulls the cuff of his jumper over his hand and wipes away the layer of dust residing on the top shelf, then brushing the residue from his arm, places the box down, pulls the lid open and immediately begins unravelling the bubble wrap engulfing the items. Once completing the last rotation, he holds the uncovered picture frame at arms reach. By chance, the picture inside faces toward the floor whilst its rear leg faces him, which provides some much needed emotional respite before revealing its contents. He turns the frame and places it upon the top, now dustless, shelf as the picture comes into clear view. His mother and father at one of their many parties, smiling and lovingly holding one another. Not posing, he thinks. They were just one of the lucky ones.

Well, apart from…

He has no time to dwell, for he knows the last two items that need to be placed, still reside in that box. Leaning back down, he takes a hold of two brushed metal urns and pulls them from their temporary cardboard dwelling.

Placing them both onto the shelf, he then adjusts their spacing to symmetrically sit either side of the frame - the engravings reading, 'Beloved Mother' and 'Beloved Father'. The moment becomes overwhelming and a surge of tears begin to form at the base of his eyes.

A floorboard creaks from behind and he quickly turns to see Nia slowly walking into the room. Always wanting to remain strong for her sake, he gives a sharp sniff and rubs the corner of his eyes, as though the countryside allergies are affecting him.

Nia may be young, but she most definitely carries an old head on those shoulders. Seeing through her brother's charade, she walks towards him and gently leans her head into his shoulder, so he can regain his doting stature and be the one to put his arm around her, which he does. They stand in silence just looking at the picture together.

Something he has shamefully only now come to realise is just how natural they were as parents - loving and supportive whilst instilling a level of authority to keep him (in their words) 'on the straight and narrow' - a perfect balance. He misses them terribly and it hurts even more due to the horrific nature of their untimely deaths, but his heartache isn't egocentric, it's empathic grief for Nia's loss. This poor girl, losing both parents at such a young age and now having to uproot her entire life to live with this complete stranger of a person she calls 'brother' - what sort of chance does she stand now?

Sensing his angst, Nia soon takes it upon herself to break the melancholia and mutters from under Dion's arm.

"Want to hear something funny to cheer you up?" she asks.

"Go on then," he replies with a smile.

"It's dark."

Dion knows that if *she* is saying the following joke is dark, then he best prepare himself.

"Just say it," he submits.

She takes one more beat then, with great indifference, utters the words, "It's funny how you can die in a house fire, and yet still be cremated."

Dion laughs, almost in disgust at himself, then mockingly shoves Nia away with one arm.

Likely due to some form of conditioning from his parents' upbringing as the 'older sibling', Dion never swears around his younger sister. But the moment feels like an exception to the rule and he can't help but exclaim, "Fucking hell Nia!"

Laughing, she replies "I warned you!"

Shaking his head and unable to look his sister in the eye, Dion focuses his attention on the box filled with remaining trinkets by his feet. Leaning, he takes a firm grip on both sides then stands tall.

"How's your unpacking going?" he asks.

"It's not."

Having given Nia the largest bedroom, Dion's feet graze the enclosed oak-panelled walls as he sits with both legs outstretched on the floor, but he doesn't mind the lack of space - a bed and cabinet is everything he needs. Leaning his back against his bed frame for support, he rummages through the array of never-ending cardboard boxes; never-ending because he can't help but reminisce over every item he pulls from inside.

Old CDs that he's not listened to in decades, but now wants nothing more than to hear their melodies, to remind himself of better times. This then means he *must* find the old stereo that he knows is packed somewhere within the abyss, in order to play said CD, which then reveals another item which he now *must* have, and so on.

Eventually noticing his reflection from the screen of a Tamagotchi, he realises his unpacking has been less than successful and decides to leave this for another day.

He walks down the long hallway and notices Nia's bedroom door slightly ajar. There, she sits crossed legged amongst a pile of unopened cardboard boxes reading a book - a familiar sight in their household. Gently knocking on the door causes it to open with a rustic creak - the discovery of her brother's looming presence startling Nia. Holding back the urge to laugh in retaliation for earlier events, Dion smiles.

"Bored yet?"

"I started bored." Nia quips.

Dion quietly thinks to himself before eventually breaking his contemplation. "Fancy taking a break and doing something fun?"

The living room provides some much needed space to an otherwise labyrinth of congestion. Its high ceilings host two sizeable antler-themed chandeliers, each offering a dim glow from only three working bulbs (out of a possible eight), which does very little in helping against the darkness of night, which now closes in. By complete contrast, the low hanging beams offer just enough height from the ground, that Nia's five-feet-four frame can feel strands of hair brush past as she walks beneath them. Dion, on the other hand, is finding himself continually knocking his head, and this is no exception, as he provides an auditory 'bang' followed by sounds of disgruntlement whilst approaching the cast-iron log burner situated in the corner of the room.

Burning an amalgamation of cardboard boxes, twigs and anything else he can use as fuel, Dion stands back and watches the dancing flames sporadically light the dull room with tiger-like orange and black stripes projecting across the walls. He soon begins to feel a warm, comforting sensation, but it's not ignited by the heat of the fire, it comes in the form of a distant memory that always finds its way to the forefront of his mind whenever he watches a fireplace - reminiscing on the time he learned to make his first fire.

A small child proudly accompanying his father on a fishing trip to Lake Windermere. Compared to his familiar urban surroundings, the mountainous terrain and wide open vistas appeared like something from one of his fantasy bedtime reads, but the excursion had taken its toll on a young Dion and as he grew weary, he clumsily fell off the boat and into the lake. Being a crisp autumn day, the water wasn't death-defyingly cold, but enough to feel the bitter pinch all over his body. Always the hero in his stories, Dion's father quickly returned them to the log cabin and comforted a cold and disheartened Dion, teaching him (not showing) how to make a fire in order to warm himself, reminding him, "The only real mistake is the one from which we learn nothing" (which Dion later discovered is a famous quote by Henry Ford - something his father omitted at the time) but it's become a prominent lesson in Dion's life and one which he continually finds himself referencing, simply due to the sheer volume of mistakes he has made.

Meanwhile, Nia sits patiently in silence, waiting for her brother to fulfil his promise of 'doing something fun' until he finally joins her, knocking his head along the way for good measure.

The house seems to provide an ever-flowing offering of curiosities, and today's discovery comes in the form of the living rooms' old coffee table, which just happens to have the engravings of a chequered board etched into its centre, and the two of them now sit comfortably across from one another playing a game of chess. After a moment of clarity, Nia cannot help but see their frivolities objectively.

"You know, this wasn't exactly what I had in mind when you said we should do something fun," she protests.

Dion laughs and retorts, "You used to love playing chess together!"

Nia jokingly ducks in embarrassment and looks around the empty space surrounding them, "Alright, no need to tell everyone!"

Laughter fills the air whilst the two of them continue with their strategic plays. Eventually the tone settles and Nia becomes increasingly introverted.

"You know it was never the chess I wanted to spend time with." Having uttered the words, Nia can't look at her brother and continues to act as though she is contemplating her next move.

The room attempts to fall into an awkward silence, but the distant sounds from the crackling fireplace manage to break what would have otherwise been an unbearable tension.

The comment fills Dion with a burden of regret. He looks up, and although she now desperately stares into the chequered board, Dion knows her words must have been hard to admit. But what can he say? He knows he should have been around more, to console her after that first heartbreak, to cheer her team on when they played in the finals - or to have just *been* there for her.

And just as he is about to admit defeat, a glimmer of hope begins to emerge, as he realises this situation has provided him with a second chance to correct all of that - but his thoughts have taken too long and Nia finally raises her head to look at him, waiting for a response that never comes.

Her expression changes to shock as she blurts, "Oh come on. I'm pouring my heart out, you can't just pull that face!"

Dion laughs awkwardly and knows he must say something to fix this moment.

"No, I know I should have been there more. It's terrible how easily you start to focus on your own life and drift apart from others. We're told *live your life. Don't worry about what other people think* - but we forget that your life isn't just your own, it's shared with others, people you care about, and who care about you, who helped define you, and whether we like it or not, the ones who truly mean something, we're all part of one, shared life experience."

Dion can see from Nia's reaction that he's managed to redeem himself, and although what he said is true, he doesn't quite understand where it came from. It must have existed as an emotion that buried itself deep inside for years, just waiting for the right time to be expressed through words.

"So, what's the plan now we're back sharing a life together?" Nia inquires.

Dion begins to recall that earlier pep talk with himself, knowing 'Step Two' is yet to appear within his master plan, and for a second he pauses with fear - not knowing how to respond. However, he soon remembers his own consolation and hoping to interject before Nia has noticed his glimpse of repose, continues, "I'm not worried about what will happen. As long as we're together, got a roof over our heads and food in our stomachs, then I'll feel like I've done something right."

They both gleam, finding themselves staring at the chessboard like a couple of Cheshire cats, all the while trying to hide their emotions from one another.

Eventually Nia breaks the silence. "Well, that just got serious very quickly."

She looks back down at the chess board and knows the perfect move to break this proverbial ice. Grasping the Queen between her fingertips, she begins to jump the piece over the top of Dion's pawn then taps it down and proceeds to repeat the motion to the remainder of his pieces, zigzagging her chess piece to the back of the board as though playing a game of chequers. On the final tap down she looks up at her brother and joyfully proclaims, "Jenga!"

Dion erupts in hysterical laughter, so loud that he can actually hear himself, and realises that Nia's laughter hasn't been the only unfamiliar sound recently. Once calm, and having dried his joyous damp eyes, Dion can see that Nia is rummaging on the top of a cabinet and eventually reveals their somewhat unfamiliar house keys.

She then clarifies, "OK, Why don't I go get us some picky bits, you know *real food*, a couple of alcoholic beverages and we'll get this party started!"

"What, on your own?" as the words leave his mouth, he already knows they were a mistake.

Worried that he may have just ruined a perfectly pleasant moment shared between them, Dion looks sheepishly toward Nia who merely gives him the solemn head tilt - a pleasant enough visual cue without too much reproach.

Noticing her candour, Dion simply smiles and nods, his own visual cue that he will try to do better.

And with that, Nia leaves the house. Now alone, Dion notices the looming shadows setting deeply across each of the walls and with a little more haste than he would like to admit, moves towards the window overlooking the front of the house to watch as Nia disappears down the lane. With the two of them having spent every waking minute together for the past week, this feels like dropping a child off for their first day of school whilst he continues to sit beside the window and wait for her return, and it's not long before he's no longer alone, except it's not Nia that's returned - it's the woman.

To ensure it's not the equivalent of seeing a coat in the middle of a darkened room and thinking it's a spectre, he blinks twice and refocuses.

But there she stands in the middle of the grounds, her dark hair and deathly white eyes highlighted by tonight's crescent moon. He jumps to attention, sprints downstairs and flings the back door crashing open as he exits out of the back entrance. Once again she has vanished, just a void of darkness now surrounds the house.

Dion stands beside the back door, his breath evaporating into wisps of cloud in the cool night air. The calm silence is soon broken as loud footsteps run behind him.

He turns to find nothing, but the footsteps continue throughout the house, leaping up the stairs and crescendoing with a loud bang as a door slams shut. Bypassing sensibility, Dion's movements are now acting on pure impulse as he darts back into the house and follows the audible trail of breadcrumbs upstairs. The trail soon ends.

The bathroom door that is currently closed, slowly begins to creep open, and the realisation begins to dawn as to which genre he is now the feature of. He knows he shouldn't enter this room, that every imaginary audience member is currently screaming at him '*don't go in there!*', but intrigue has got the better of him.

He walks cautiously toward the bathroom, raising his hand to slowly push the door wide open before stepping inside. Nothing is out of place, the shower gel sits on the bathtub side, the soap comfortably in its holder and his toothpaste and brush reside just where he left them, although the mirror seems slightly ajar. And as soon as he pushes the angle back into place he immediately regrets his decision. He can now see his own reflection staring back at him - and the space behind him. Fortunately, that's all that stands behind him - empty space. He breathes a sigh of relief, half expecting the woman to have filled that void in the mirror, concluding he has watched too many horror films.

He turns to leave and the woman's face now fills his vision as her piercing white eyes stare an inch from his. Opening her mouth she exhales a high pitch screech which sends Dion flying back and landing hard on the tiled floor. As he regains composure an arm grabs his shoulder and violently shakes him.

"Dion!"

He looks up to find a concerned Nia kneeling over him but even her presence isn't enough to overcome his current level of fear.

"Dion! Are you OK?" she pleads.

Dion feels rational thought seeping back and he can finally formulate a sentence.

"Yea, yea. No I'm fine. Just slipped."

Nia looks around at the empty floor.

"On what?"

Dion also looks down, trying to find something to corroborate his story but is also at a loss.

"Just. Slipped?"

Nia stares deep into his eyes trying to find truth in what he says. Knowing this, Dion dawns his best pokerface and sits in hope that the expression does enough to protect him against any follow-up questions. A few moments of silence pass until she finally breaks.

"I leave for five bloody minutes!" she laughs.

Dion laughs, more than he should, as fear and relief exude through his rhythmic chuckling. Offering both hands, Nia helps Dion to his feet.

"Well, not that it looks like you need any, but let's go crack these bottles open!" she jests.

Nia then heads downstairs, leaving Dion alone with his thoughts, too petrified to move.

He hasn't had a chance to fully digest these recurring visions. Again, he had assumed after all that happened to them, the moving, the long drive down, that possibly (and most likely) his mind was playing tricks on him the day he first saw the woman - but twice, well shame on him for not thinking something is terribly wrong. Now, faith isn't something that has ever come naturally to Dion, no matter how much his parents tried to instil Christianity within their household, (he even remembers raising his hand to ask a question amidst a Sunday service as a child and being lambasted for it) so to his atheist mind, ghosts, spectres, spirits, are all part of the same imaginary nonsense, just people draped in bedsheets with eye holes cut out. So that quite firmly eliminates all possibility of this woman being of the occult. Which makes him feel much better, momentarily. So then, what is she? If not something extrinsic projecting *at* him then, by process of elimination, it must be something intrinsically projecting itself *to* him. Which terrifies Dion far more than any ghost story ever could. He decides to solve the situation in the only way he knows how.

He walks away to enjoy his time with Nia, and forgets about it.

A concoction of half-empty glasses, beer bottles, crips and sweet wrappers are now spread across the kitchen table as Dion clears everything away into a black bin liner - a good night on all accounts - but a sense of melancholia soon overcomes him whilst standing alone in the quiet room that was filled with laughter and reminiscent anecdotes less than thirty-minutes ago.

He soon washes up the dirty glasses, slightly too inebriated to even begin comprehending the frightful events earlier that night, then eventually heads to bed. Walking down the hallway whilst trying to find his sea legs, Dion notices Nia's door slightly ajar and it brings an instant smile to his face. She still likes keeping her door open after all these years.

As Nia grows older, he finds it increasingly harder to relate to this adult version of her and not the child he knew so well - not in an unpleasant way, for he loves the person she has become, but just noticing something she's kept from their childhood brings a much needed sense of familiarity.

Ignoring the natural urge to close the door, he continues down the hallway and into his room, where he falls straight to sleep.

Dion soon awakes in total darkness, his head spinning from the slight excess of drinks last night. He rolls over to try and catch a glimpse of the time but something is blocking the bedside table.

No. Not something. *Someone* he doesn't recognise.

3

I raise my head, following the silhouetted outline of a figure. The woman is here, stood at my bedside staring at me once again. But something's different. Even in the darkness I can see her eyes, not those soulless white spheres, her actual eyes. They're beautiful. They take me by surprise until the realisation dawns on me as to what is happening and I scuttle backwards across the bed, when suddenly she speaks.

"Dion?"

The way she calls my name is so warming, inviting even, but it doesn't lessen the fear of waking up to a stranger standing beside you in the middle of the night. As soon as I hit the floor, I scramble to my feet but my legs are still half asleep, as is my head, and I falter.

I slam my back into the wall to help keep me upright, the woman just watching the entire time.

"Dion? It's OK Dion."

There it is, my name again, but how?

I notice a lamp sat on the bedside table just a few feet from my position. Using the wall as a support, I roll to one side and flick the switch. Although a weak bulb, the sudden glow causes momentarily blindness until my eyes finally adapt and see her. All of her. Her flowing dark hair, her dark brown eyes, her rouge lips. Just as I'm becoming more acquainted with this new version of her, she turns and begins walking towards me, and that I am most definitely not ready for.

"Dion! It's OK, you're here with me now. Everything's going to be alright." What is she talking about?

There isn't time to think, she's gaining on me and I need to awaken these dead legs before she gets any closer. With every ounce of strength, I push off the wall and manage to balance on both legs before scurrying for the door, but it's not quite where it should be. Actually, nothing is. The cabinet is on the wrong side of the room, there's no moving boxes, and the lamp I just turned on shouldn't even be there. My head begins to pound like a blacksmith hammering an anvil and in an attempt to lessen the pain, I bring both hands to my temple. A temple that's now covered in long, scraggly hair. Panicking, I begin to lower my hands, which now brush past a bearded face.

I rush to a mirror situated in the corner of the room to reveal a version of myself that I don't recognise. It's most definitely me; when I hold up this hand, he responds with the same gesture, and when I blink, the world falls into evanescent darkness before returning to life, and there he is.

That pain once again forking itself across my temple.

"What's happening!? Where am I?" the words leave my mouth before I even have a chance to articulate.

"Dion, it's OK. You've been gone a long time, but you're back here with me now." The woman is calming me with a gentle hand placed on the back of my neck.

The soft touch feels incredible and I just want to fall into this stranger's arms and be told that everything is going to be alright, but the moment quickly passes when the image of Nia flashes into my head.

My legs are now fully operational and I throw open the door, hurrying down the hallway to Nia's bedroom, but her door is not how I left it.

It's closed tight.

Reaching out, I take a hold of the handle, click down and release. The door flies open as the hallway light beams across the floor.

The room is empty.

No sign of Nia's presence, or anyone else's for that matter. The woman has now caught up to me and as she approaches I spin to confront her.

"Where's my sister!?"

She looks at me with complete bemusement.

"Your sister?" she asks.

Like a Mexican standoff in the hallway, we just stare at one another, neither wanting to break first.

"She's not here. No one is." The woman finally clarifies.

No.

What starts as a jog, increases to a run, which escalates into a sprint throughout the house.

"Nia!"

Opening every door.

"Nia!"

Searching every room.

"Nia!"

Looking round every corner.

Suddenly I find myself outside in the middle of the grounds as the sun is rising. Apart from some distant trees blocking a tiny area of perspective, the surrounding vista is entirely flat, allowing for sweeping panoramic views of the countryside for miles. Only the stream running beside the house can be heard at this hour with its gentle wet hum echoing into the stark pink sky - it's the type of setting that would make for an incredible sight if it weren't for the nightmare I am currently facing. Once again the woman has caught up to me and I finally concede. My legs give way and I crumple to the ground, the smell of fresh soil soaked in morning dew providing my only solace.

Kneeling beside me, the woman speaks softly in my ear.

"It's OK Dion, just breathe."

I almost fall under her spell, but an uncontrollable anger ignites inside of me and erupts.

"What is this!? Who are you!?"

Tears fill my eyes as I gaze deep into hers, but she remains calm, if not sporting a hint of woe. Lowering herself onto the ground, we now sit beside one another at complete equal heights as she continues to explain, "I don't know how much you remember, or if you are even aware of what's happening right now?"

I shake my head.

"What do you remember, exactly?" she follows up.

I think before responding, knowing what she means by the question, but equally having no idea how to respond.

"After the house burned down. We inherited this place and temporarily living here was the only logical thing to do for Nia."

Her head dips slightly and her voice is getting a little quieter.

"I've been dreading having to explain this to you. But. Dion. Your entire family died that night in the house fire."

I look at her, a little unsure as to what she's implying. When she says 'family' I assume she's speaking in reference to my dear parents who lost their lives in that tragic house fire; the fire that destroyed both our lives, our childhood home and brought us to this place. But I can feel her assessing my thoughts and before I can get ahead of myself, she cautiously continues.

"Everyone. Including Nia."

My world just fell apart.

"No. No she couldn't have. I was *just* with her." I tell myself out loud.

"Can you explain exactly where that was?" the question feels so ridiculous that I respond in a manner that is directed far too bitterly at someone being so kind.

"Here! In this house!"

"I see." she pauses. It's the first time I have seen her pondering over words. She soon calculates the correct response and continues.

"Would you like to know what really happened?"

"That *is* what happened!" her hurt is evident as I lambast, but I feel my irritation has merit.

We both sit in silence, and I'm certain it's for the same reason - this situation is absurd and only one of us can be correct. I look out and watch as the sunrise slowly grows brighter in the morning sky and casts a foreboding shadow over the house, when suddenly our mutual silence is broken by a familiar voice.

"Dion!" Nia's cry echoes across the landscape.

I knew it couldn't be true. I rise to my feet and respond, "Nia!"

The woman quickly stands to attention beside me, staring with worrying eyes.

"Dion." She cautions.

I ignore her concern and continue to make my way across the grounds as I hear Nia's voice calling once again.

"Dion!"

It's getting closer but I can't see her. Where is she? The woman is gaining proximity on me and tries to reach out a hand to hold my shoulder but I manage to shoo it away.

"Dion, please."

The thought occurs like a streak of lightning hitting only once. Who is this woman? Is she dangerous? How did she get into our house? Not wanting to lead her one step closer to Nia, I turn to confront her. But she is no longer there.

Instead, Nia's teary blue eyes now look into mine.

4

Dion's legs falter and he collapses into Nia's arms as they embrace - Dion holding so tightly that his hands meet behind her back. If there has ever been a more joyous moment shared between the two of them, he certainly can't remember it anymore. As his face brushes the side of Nia's cheek he notices something is missing. He quickly touches his jaw and revels in the realisation that his face is once again clean shaven and his hair is short.

"Are you OK?" she asks.

Regaining composure, he stands and looks deep into her eyes, not knowing how to begin explaining, well, any of it. This quickly reminds him and he turns, scanning the grounds for any sign of the woman, but she's vanished once again. He begins to enquire amongst his own thoughts; She felt so real this time? Was it a dream? Was he sleepwalking? Too many questions flood his head, like standing up too quickly after sitting down. He takes Nia by the hand and begins walking them back into the safety of the house.

With great caution, Dion visually sweeps every darkened corner and slowly guides them through the back door and upstairs into the living room. Finally feeling somewhat safe, he releases his grip from Nia's hand, which was apparently far too tight judging by the tender way she now handles her fingers. But he's in too much of a frenzy to notice.

Pacing the floor back and forth, he begins to voyeur out of every window, fearing he'll catch another glimpse of the woman. All clear.

"So. Shall we talk about this?" Nia asks timidly.

Almost forgetting her presence, Dion spins with a startle. All he can muster is a blank stare.

"Or under the carpet, buried emotions, scarring us for eternity and never to be spoken of again?" she jests, trying to calm the situation.

He looks up as she raises her hands in submission and continues, "I'm good either way. It's your funeral."

Having not felt calm long enough to rationalise what he just experienced, Dion can only summarise in blurts, "I don't know? A dream, perhaps?"

Nia's expression changes to one of disbelief, something Dion has never witnessed firsthand, and a flooding of shame overcomes him.

"It was more than a dream, Dion." She deduces.

At this very moment there are a million and one things Dion doesn't know, but he certainly doesn't know what she means by this. It must have been a dream, he assumes. Taking too long to respond, Nia interrupts his thoughts.

"Would you like to know what really happened?" that same question asked by the woman outside. It must be a coincidence, he assumes again. The question soon reveals itself to be rhetorical as Nia begins to elaborate.

"You were having some kind of night terror - thanks for that by the way, nothing like waking up to screaming in the 'House on Haunted Hill' - then you awoke in some kind of daze," she pauses briefly to think how best to describe it, "like sleepwalking, except it wasn't - it was as though you were both asleep *and* awake. I kept trying to wake you, but you just strolled around the house muttering to yourself about some woman, and then went galavanting outside."

The words unfold as though Dion's life is being narrated to him, but not how he remembers it. Never one to wear his heart on his sleeve, Dion knows he needs to explain everything before losing Nia's faith forever. He guides them over to the table where they, just last night, shared that happy memory of playing chess together. Now, again trying to preempt how best to position his pieces, Dion decides to just speak as the thoughts come to him.

"That woman. The one I was muttering about. I've been having visions of her," his voice trails off.

Unsure how to react, Nia digresses with humour, "We'll come back to that, but go on."

He continues, "Then one night, she's just standing there at the foot of my bed and suddenly I'm here. But not *here*. It was so familiar, and so unfamiliar."

He can feel his thoughts failing him, knowing this speech is causing more harm than good, but he continues in vain.

"She said," his voice trailing once again as the sudden revelation of the woman's words reverberate within Dion's mind '*Everyone. Including Nia.*'

Pausing, he knows rationality must now dictate his words and he segues into a different tact, "And then we're taking a stroll outside and I heard your voice. And now, well."

"But who was she?"

"I don't know, but she sure knew me," trying to divert the conversation, Dion elaborates, "every tiny detail of this place was the same, except, it was as though I was looking at it through a mirror."

Nia can see a dangerous disconnect forming in his eyes and she asks, "But you do know *this* is real, right? Here and now, with me?"

Dion nods, continuing to look at the ground.

"I know how this sounds." He answers sadly.

"No, I believe you. I just don't know what we do now, do you need help?"

The worrying notion that his little sister is having to take care of him in this way causes him more concern than the actual thought of needing therapy, and he finally looks up to tell her straight. But the woman is stood inches behind Nia's shoulder, her white eyes once again burning into Dion's.

He ejects from his chair with a scream.

"What!?" Nia shouts whilst looking behind her.

As quick as she appeared, the woman has once again vanished and Dion now stands whilst hyperventilating.

"It's her isn't it? The woman?" Nia questions.

"No"

"Can you see her now?" Nia continues.

"It's nothing."

"Dion!" Nia pleads.

"NIA STOP!"

The anger, the fear, the sorrow, the pain. Everything has overflown like a boiling pot and Dion knows he can never take this moment back. He instantly feels remorse and tries to reconcile by holding out his hand to hug her, but Nia shrugs him away and storms out of the room, leaving Dion completely alone.

Trying to diffuse the pain, Dion brings both hands up to his face and grips tightly as he screams into his palms.

The large wooden dining table now supports the weight of a no-expenses-spared roast dinner, which spreads itself from either end with more food than a family of five could ever consume - Dion's shameless (and failed) attempt at forgiveness.

Dion and Nia sit opposite one another in the dimly lit kitchen and painfully eat in awkward silence, the shrill of their metallic cutlery on porcelain plates providing the only audible respite to tonight's proceedings.

Eventually becoming too familiar with the silence, Dion offers some of his best comedy, "Nice weather we've been having?"

Nothing. Not even a glance. He tries again, this time dawning an American accent to enhance the performance, "How 'bout those dodgers?"

A slight raise of the eyebrow, but still not enough to satisfy Dion's desire to be forgiven, suddenly it dawns on him and he knows the perfect movie quote for this situation, "This one time, at band camp!"

Finally she breaks and, albeit small, Nia gives a feint laugh but quickly regains composure.

"No Dion, we can't just sweep this under the carpet."

"No I know, I,"

Nia quickly interrupts, "It's happening again isn't it?"

He stares at Nia with complete bewilderment. Again?

"What, no, I've never?" He asks.

Slowly sinking into herself, she finally elaborates. "Mum explained everything."

Dion cannot fathom what this could possibly mean. What is happening again? This has never happened before. Has it?

Too many questions all at once start making his head pound. Except the pounding isn't coming from a migraine. It's coming from the front door.

He looks toward the door with total confusion as to who this could be, not just at this hour, but at this house. No one knows they are here.

He turns to Nia - a panicked expression now forming across her face.

"Nia?" Dion asks with deep concern.

"I'm so sorry, I'm so sorry" Nia forfeits and stands, heading out of the room.

"Nia?" Dion repeats, this time with more fear than concern in his voice as he follows down the hallway.

"You won't talk to me! I didn't know what else to do, I didn't know who else to call!" she cries whilst continuing to head for the door, reaching out her hand.

"Nia!" Dion shouts as Nia quickly opens the door. She beams a smile at someone and leans forward to hug whoever is currently being obstructed by the large oak door blocking Dion's view. He leans to one side, trying to get a better look when the stranger finally enters.

It's the woman. The same woman who has been haunting his thoughts from the moment they arrived at this house. In the blink of an eye, her confident strides suddenly begin closing in on Dion and he tries to retreat but soon comes to a crashing standstill as his back slams against the solid wall behind him. There's nowhere to escape and he can only watch as her hypnotic brown eyes dance towards him.

It's too much to bear and Dion can feel his head spinning out of control as his legs give way and everything fades to black.

5

As though suspended in animation, the surrounding world begins to fall away as I land heavily onto the floor. Finally, my head regains a sense of orientation and I can see the woman rushing towards me, but once again Nia is nowhere to be seen.

"No, no no!" I cry.

"Dion, please calm down, it's me, remember?" she pleads.

"What is happening!?"

Placing a confiding hand on my shoulder she continues, "It's OK, the confusion you're feeling is completely normal."

I'm not sure what she deems as normal, but this most certainly is not it.

"Did you see her again? Nia? You were talking about her," she questions.

Pushing off the floor I gain a stronger stance and shout, "Yes! She was just standing right there! She let you in!"

"Please calm down."

I ignore this and yell as loud as my throat can bear.

"Nia!"

"Dion, please," she interrupts, with an air of embarrassment.

I continue, "Nia!" the rasp in my voice gives way before I can fully expel her last vowel.

The silence answers my call and I begin to concede.

"What is this?"

As soon as my question hangs in the air, I decide defeat is not an option, and I begin searching for my sister.

An empty hallway leads me up the stairs to an empty living room. There's not a single remnant of Nia anywhere, the chessboard no longer engraved within the table, and everything seems to be located in areas it shouldn't be. The only items that seem to have remained are the urns I placed on that top shelf. Of course they would survive this ordeal, just one more tragedy to weigh on this camel's back.

One striking feature that's now found solace in this room is a large freestanding mirror. A desire to see my own reflection overcomes me and I edge closer before seeing that same unrecognisably unkempt version of myself. I cannot look at him for more than a second, then think it's probably time to check Nia's bedroom, although I am slowly surrendering to the truth that she will not be there. Which she isn't.

Returning to the kitchen, the woman is now seated at the dining table, looking up at me with those dark brown eyes.

"You're still here?" I ask rhetorically.

"And so are you."

I've been running away from problems my entire life, and today is going to be no exception to that rule. Without another word spoken, I turn and leave the room.

Wandering aimlessly through the meandering hallways, I soon decide there is little reason to escape and so I head to my bedroom and notice the remains of last night's awakening, the unmade bed from where I threw off the duvet, the scattering of furniture from which I bulldozed my way through - that lurid instant just frozen in time.

Screeching the side table back to its original position and floating the duvet onto the mattress, the room begins to resemble how I imagine it looked prior to my antics - although, it still feels like I'm occupying someone else's room. Sitting on the edge of my bed, I stare out of the window and begin to contemplate what life is going to be like should this all turn out to be true, but soon enough, an overbearing tiredness shackles me to the bed and I slowly begin to drift.

Awakening with some hopefulness that this may have all been one cliched dream - the beard on my face and incorrect positioning of everything in my room confirms I am still here. Wherever that may be. A golden scent of toast ignites my hunger and I follow its aroma into the kitchen. The woman is still here, reading a newspaper and drinking an extremely pale looking coffee, all the while staring at me with the most unbearably pleasant smile one could imagine at a time like this.

"Well, good morning!" the voice matches her expression.

The word 'morning' repeats itself.

"It's tomorrow?" I ask.

"Well, compared to yesterday, yes."

She's far too chipper.

I avert her stare and notice the fresh spread of fruits, toast and orange juice laid out on the table.

"Coffee?" she asks.

"Please."

As she walks over to the cafetiere sat beside the kettle, I take the opportunity to slip into the seat furthest away. Whilst watching the coffee steadily pour, a burning question gets the better of me.

"So, I was down all day and night?"

"Well, it was quite the day yesterday, I'm sure you needed your rest."

Not the direct answer I was looking for, but I think that confirms I slept through the whole day. I begin spreading some butter across the perfectly brown toast as she takes a seat and passes across the cup. I stare down into the well of deep aromatic coffee and hesitate. It's *exactly* how I like it. Maybe she really does know me?

The room falls to a peaceful quiet before being interrupted by her questioning, "Is there anything you would like to ask?"

"What is this? Therapy?" what should have been a joke, comes out with far more venom than I ever intended, and I immediately want to retract. Although, she seems to accept it in the manner I originally intended.

"Well *this,*" she responds, pointing at me then back to herself, "is not no. But *this,*" she continues raising both hands to emphasise everything around us at this moment in time, "*this* is. Yes."

I hold a single piece of toast mid-air in total awe of her complete disregard for sensing tone.

"Can you please just tell me what is going on?" I ask.

She smiles, as though she's happy I've finally stumbled on the correct question.

"OK, Dion, let me explain. And if at any point this feels like too much, you just tell me to stop." Her tone is like that of a school teacher before explaining something 'wasn't your fault'.

"After you lost everyone in the fire, you had a complete, well, we don't like to call it this anymore, but for lack of a better term, you had a complete 'mental breakdown'."

My mind races but I say nothing.

"You went into something of a comatose state and were brought here for rehabilitation, with me as your live-in help and therapist - sorry where are my manners."

She holds out her hand, and the realisation that this is to request a handshake takes me longer to comprehend than I care to admit.

"I'm Dr Minos."

She has a name, an identity - but for reasons I can't explain, this doesn't seem to make her any more real. Finally reciprocating the gesture, I squeeze firmly whilst her gentle grip feels warm and inviting, then release as she continues.

"And, as for where you've been."

This is one step too far on our journey of self-discovery and I cut her off mid-sentence.

"I know where I've been."

The room falls silent once again and as she takes a cumbrous sip of coffee I can feel my face scowl. Except this time I mean it.

6

As time passes, so does my desire to stay here. Well, not here in this house, but here *together*. Dr Minos seems entirely pleasant but we are complete strangers cohabiting my family's heirloom property, which I am told is accurate, one of the few things I have remembered correctly, apparently.

Each morning I awake, walk the grounds whilst the sun gleams its vibrant autumn colours across the sky, commence our uncomfortable breakfasts with iterations of 'whenever you're ready', which I never am nor ever will be, then continue my day of reading the daily newspaper, completing (attempting) its crossword, further walking of the grounds, dinner followed by even more awkwardness for desert, a little light reading from whatever I find occupying the bookshelves, then fall into a restless slumber. And repeat.

Until now, I have been simply floating in a sea of obscurity and waiting for that moment where I click my red shoes three times and find myself reunited with Nia. But today I feel different.

Having spent much longer walking this morning, I had even more time to think, which is comic irony at its finest considering that's all I ever do here, but today I noticed something whilst walking beside the narrow stretch of river that runs adjacent to the house. With great tranquility the water flows in graceful unison along the main path, but then an obstruction appears in the form of a small island coated in wiry foliage. Without any resistance, the river's path seamlessly reroutes in two directions, continuing to flow either side of the bank before returning to meet at the end and peacefully continue its journey. Granted, I've clearly had far too much time on my hands to associate such a common occurrence with any sort of life lesson, but it struck me that even if this whole situation is one odd detour and my path will eventually reunite me with Nia and we live happily ever after - then I need to just continue flowing with the current, not fighting against it and making the final destination take even longer to approach. And so I decide to embrace this reality, identify the obstruction my mind is clearly trying to alert me of, and start to appease Dr Minos' requests.

Returning to the kitchen I realise my longer than usual walk has thrown off Dr Minos' schedule and she's nowhere to be seen, and so I make a small black cup of coffee and stand by the window overlooking the grounds - that rich aroma igniting my senses whilst I contemplate every possible outcome to the questions I'm now forming. Once content, I place the empty cup down.

The living room was also empty and so I now climb the winding staircase to the snug area which hovers at the highest point of the house, where I finally find Dr Minos engulfed by the high angular beams whilst sitting on a crimson leather armchair, a broadsheet newspaper covering her face. I begin to awkwardly drift my gaze across the room, and having not been up here much, I notice it's an extremely pleasant area to sit - the bannisters overlooking the living room below provide a unique view of the house that I've never noticed before and the lack of any windows make the room's dismal lighting an ideal location to withdraw oneself. Unsure as to what my next move should be, I continue over to a seat at the far end of the room and pretend to make myself comfortable, in a most uncomfortable position. A list of burning questions now weigh like a heavy burden, and I haven't the slightest idea as to how I begin asking them. I hope to catch a glance of her looking over but she keeps the broadsheet (quite literally) close to her chest.

The weight of questions finally unbalance and my words escape before I've even acknowledged them, "OK so what are we meant to be doing here?"

Dr Minos immediately lowers the broadsheet to reveal a huge smile, like a hammock hanging from ear to ear, clearly preempting this.

"Well, funnily enough, you're already sitting in my 'therapy chair' over there. Or 'chaise longue' if you want to be pretentious."

I don't.

"OK, well, don't get any ideas!" my attempt to break the tension with humour.

It's the first time she's laughed at something I've said and it feels surprisingly nice.

"I wouldn't dream of it!" she projects from across the room, "and to be completely honest, it's a lot of *this* really. Talking through your emotions, your thoughts."

Pausing there, I'm certain she's posing the open-ended response as a means to reel me into the conversation.

I bite.

"So, let's say I was intrigued to hear your thoughts on 'where I've been'."

"Well," she stands and takes one step towards me.

Holding up my hand I respond.

"No no, still in hypotheticals here."

She smiles sweetly and almost curtsies herself back into her seat.

"OK, well *hypothetically* I would assume where you've been was some form of 'Double Bookkeeping' or 'Derealisation', where you've created a reality inside of your own mind. A reality where you feel safe. Where Nia didn't perish and you were able to live in peace knowing you saved her and could care for her. Masking the trauma of what actually happened."

They say that truth hurts, and so the resounding pain deep inside my chest is all the clarification I need. As much as I can't remember this reality ever happening, it now feels just as real as when I was with Nia. Maybe I have been living a curated life? But what is preventing *this* reality from also being a creation of my mind? And, in essence, isn't that all reality is - a complex interpretation of what our minds deem as 'real'? I've never been one for art, but a distant memory that I was unaware even existed, has decided to surface itself. As with the majority of things one becomes educated on during their school years, I was never certain why we learned it, but for whatever reason the curriculum dictated that we needed to know about surrealist painters and my mind's eye cannot stop picturing Magritte's painting 'The Treachery of Images'. It's such a simple painting featuring an old brown pipe with the words 'Ceci n'est pas une pipe' (This is not a pipe) written below, and it never truly resonated with me until this very moment. Am I the pipe? Or the painting of a pipe?

Existential questions soon disperse and are replaced with visions of Nia. If what Dr Minos says is true, then I have already lost my only purpose in life.

I return to myself and find that I'm becoming teary whilst idly staring through the bannisters and out of the large window in the distance. How simple life seems when you look at the vast beauty surrounding it. Before having a chance to recuperate, Dr Minos is sat beside me with her gentle touch on my shoulder.

"I know this must be an extraordinary amount to bear. But the first thing I need you to understand, Dion, is that none of what happened was your fault."

The sensation in my eyes means I have seconds before the seal is broken and I know Dr Minos can sense it too.

"I think that's enough for one day." She says squeezing my shoulder before taking her leave.

The tears come soon after.

The rising sun finds its way into my bedroom and paints the walls with a golden hue. This is the highlight of my day, awakening before comprehension has taken its hold, and in that split second, hope prevails. But it's short lived and is soon followed by the sinking realisation that today is another day in this reality.

As I leave the room and echo my footsteps through the long hallway, something catches my attention beside me. It's that same picture of the Victorian woman posing for a photo, although this time the frame hangs on the wall and remains intact. I lean closer to investigate and can see the burn marks remain deeply set across her eyes. This entire home is filled with nondescript pictures hanging on the wall, all of which I take no notice of, and if it weren't for my brief encounter with this precise image then it would have just blurred into the rest of the crowd - but it hasn't. Why this picture? Why did I conjure this into some form of consciousness with such affliction? Or is it just something I noticed in passing and this entire exercise is fruitless? After much deliberation, I decide to ignore either outcome and continue down the hallway.

Amidst completing my morning lap of the grounds, I turn to find Dr Minos walking towards me and after our customary pleasantries, we continue the route together alongside the canal. I'm certain this was her plan, but it matters not, and I decide to explore everything a little deeper.

"Where I was, with my sister, it felt more like home. I have memories there of what happened before, whereas *here*. Nothing." I explain.

She nods politely and responds.

"The mind is a powerful tool, and even more powerful when you're unaware of what it's doing subconsciously. But we need to make you understand what *is*, and *is not*, real." She stops walking and turns to face me.

"Imagine standing in front of a mirror, you can see yourself and your surroundings, but you can also see your *same* self and your *same* surroundings in the reflection. The difference being, you are aware of the fact that where you are standing is reality, and what you're looking at is a reflection."

It feels like the perfect analogy for what I'm feeling, even better than Magritte's pipe, except one finite detail.

"But how do you know you're not the reflection?" I ask.

And for the first time she is lost for words, which pains me because I truly meant for this one not to be rhetorical - but how do you answer an unanswerable question, I suppose.

Catching me unawares she suddenly asks, "There is something I think would help if you'd be happy to oblige?"

Returning to the snug room in the uppermost section of the house, I sit on the pretentious 'chaise longue' with Dr Minos beside me in her armchair - the whole atmosphere taking a very professional turn, but I'm intrigued and start to find a more comfortable position. Head back, legs outstretched, and interlinking both hands politely across my chest.

She begins, "Now, hypnotherapy has a great track record of helping patients regain some of their memories."

The word hypnotherapy terrifies me and I sit up from what was a very relaxed position.

"Hold up, hypnotherapy? As in *hypnotising* me?" I ask fearfully.

"Yes but,"

"I don't want you in my head, making me cluck like a chicken and all that." I rather crudely exhume.

She offers a clinical smile and continues whilst gently lowering me back down into the chair.

"No, nothing like that. Hypnosis puts you into a controlled and relaxed state of mind, where we may boost the mental performance of your subconscious, and start to regain some of those memories you've, well, not *lost*, but *misplaced*, shall we say."

The blank expression currently residing on my face must clearly inform her that the explanation made no sense and so she continues.

"Think of your subconscious as your 'All-Seeing Eye', a part of your mind which is always watching and taking notes, even when your conscious is unaware of it. I'm sure you've been able to recall a fact or some sort of information without knowing where it came from?"

I nod like a petrified schoolboy.

"*That* is your subconscious mind relaying just a sliver of information to your conscious-self. The problem is, your conscious and subconscious mind have trouble communicating with one another. Therefore by putting you under hypnosis, we can improve communication between the two much more easily, and then travel back into the memories stored within your *subconscious* and bring those to the surface so that they become *conscious* memories."

She's good, slowly winning me over with every word, but my optimism is soon followed by an overwhelming sense of hesitancy.

"But what if they're memories I don't want to remember?" I fret and Dr Minos reassuringly agrees with the nod of her head.

"Some memories are harder to access than others, but whether you want to remember them or not, they are all stored in there somewhere." She says whilst pointing at the top of my head.

I ponder on my earlier revelation involving the rerouting river and finally accept her professional opinion, lowering my head onto the backrest. The moment is feeling a little too tense and so, taking a leaf from Nia's book, I try diffusing the situation with a little light humour.

"Whilst you're in there, see if you can find where I left me keys would ya?"

That warming laugh again.

"Now, close your eyes and let yourself relax completely," she instructs.

I slowly wrestle my body back into that once comfortable position, place my hands across my chest and close my eyes.

As the darkness ensues, she begins speaking in a quiet, calming tone, "Just take a deep breath in, and exhale, and as you do, just let go and relax. Let your mind relax and all your thoughts - and let your body relax and all your muscles, nerves and bones."

I can feel it working, her tranquil voice alone is enough to put me to sleep.

"Now I'm going to count from five to one, and you'll be able to go even deeper. Five, going much deeper now, four, doubling or even tripling your relaxation, three, very peaceful and relaxed, two, even more relaxed now, and one, nice and comfortable and very, very deep."

And they are the last words I hear before falling into a serene slumber.

7

Still laid out comfortably across the chaise longue, Dion can feel his heavy breathing creating tidal-like movements as his chest rises and falls. Dr Minos' voice has now stopped and he awaits eagerly for her next set of instructions, but they never come. Slowly he begins to open his eyes.

Dr Minos is no longer sat in the armchair beside him, in fact, the armchair is no longer there. Did he sleep through the whole thing? Raising his head in haste, Dion turns to find the blurred outline of a figure coming towards him. Blinking to clear his vision, the hazed image of Nia watching him slowly comes into focus. The tears in her eyes and relieved smile are overwhelming and he finally sits upright as Nia throws herself and her arms around him. Reunited at last.

"You've got to stop doing that to me!" Nia cries in his ear - the deafening sensation providing such vehemence that Dion immediately forgets everything that has since passed and finds himself simply revelling in her presence.

Eventually Nia gently releases Dion and stands tall, wiping a tear from her cheek. With great optimism Dion begins to wonder, could it be - has he finally broken through the looking glass and returned home?

"See I told you he would be OK!" Nia shouts over her shoulder.

Who is she talking to?

Dion edges his way towards the end of the seat and finds Dr Minos stood a few feet behind Nia, smiling sweetly at him - but it's not the same smile he has come accustomed to, and all hopefulness dwindles. She is almost unrecognisable with her long dark hair now tied back in a ponytail, whilst wearing a beige trench coat he's never seen before. He can't help but stare with puzzled unfamiliarity, which quickly causes her alarm.

"Dion?" she asks.

Dion rises to his feet, unable to take his eyes off her.

"Dion, are you OK?" she asks again.

"What, what are you doing here?" he utters.

"Well, to take care of you, of course!" Dr Minos replies, rather taken aback.

Unable to tell if she is who he now knows her to be, he questions, "Doctor Minos?"

Nia and Dr Minos both laugh simultaneously and look at one another with an odd expression.

"Doctor bleedin' Minos? Dion it's me!" she joyfully exclaims.

But the smiles and laughter soon culminate, fading to a display of concern. Dr Minos takes a step toward him.

"You really don't know who I am, do you?"

Looking up to find those deep brown eyes in such pain causes Dion to lose his words and instead shamefully shakes his head. He can't bear to upset her, but it's inevitable, and she takes a seat on the closest surface to calm her nerves, pausing atop an old dusty cabinet whilst catching her breath.

"Look, I don't mean to upset you, I just don't know what's going on?" asks Dion inadvertently.

Taking one last deep breath, Dr Minos rises to her feet and walks towards him, softly placing the palms of her hands on either side of his face, guiding his vision towards hers.

"Dion, look at me."

They stare into one another's eyes and Dion can see the glimmer of hope that he is about to destroy, and in desperation she tries one last time. "Dion, it's me?"

Failing to hide his bemused expression, Dr Minos' turns away, bringing her hand to her mouth.

"You honestly don't know?" Nia interjects from across the room.

Looking over at Nia then back again at Dr Minos, Dion tries to explain, "You're Doctor Minos, my Therapist, right?"

The overbearing hurt leaves Dr Minos unable to respond and Nia takes control of the situation, calmingly positioning herself between the two, in an attempt to provide Dr Minos with a moment of reprieve.

"Well, yeah, she's 'Dr Minos'. But she's not your Therapist, Dion. She's *Aria*. Your wife."

Fear, anger, heartache, confusion - all a vortex of emotions now starting to entrap Dion as he stands to reach her, but his legs waver.

"No, you're,"

His vision becomes blurry and the world around him starts to unbalance. Suddenly he hears the echoing of Dr Minos' voice, but not the one stood before him, the one residing over his hypnosis.

"*Dion. Dion are you OK?*" Her voice reverberates around the room.

He begins to sway as Nia and Dr Minos rush over and take a hold of either arm, trying to keep him upright in vain.

"No, this can't,"

He fumbles across the room reaching for anything to support his frame whilst knocking ornaments off the side cabinets as they hurtle to the ground with a smash.

"*Dion, I'm going to count from one and when I reach number five, you're going to wake up,*" that booming voice echoing inside his mind again.

Still trying to regain his footing, Dion can only rest his wearying body onto Nia and Dr Minos who continue struggling to hold him.

"*One, moving your feet and your toes, two, moving your hands and your fingers, three, lots of energy returning to the body, four, coming back to this place, this time, five, opening your eyes,*"

He hesitates with an expectation that something would awaken him, but the expectancy quickly vanishes as he looks on with hopelessness. Heaving himself forward, Dion stumbles whilst trying to escape from the room's grasp on him, when Dr Minos calls out, "Dion!"

He turns as Dr Minos lunges, grabbing either side of his arms and begins to vigorously shake him. His vision blurs and in the hope of preventing himself from vomiting, he closes both eyes tightly - plunging himself into a void of darkness.

8

The room's velocity slowly begins to dwell within the darkness, as does the nausea. I ease my eyes open to find Dr Minos' face mere inches from mine, I assume to assess consciousness judging by the flickering of her stare between both of my eyes.

"Dion it's OK, look at me."

I can feel the warmth of her soft touch on either side of my face as she guides my head towards hers.

"Are you OK? Dion?"

The remnants of discourse begin to flood my memory and her name just flows from my lips, "Aria."

She immediately releases my face and I almost fall forwards as the weight of my head unbalances without the support from her hands. I see the murmuring of tears beginning to glass over her eyes whilst she brings one hand to her gasping mouth.

"You're my wife?" I ask.

The tears now fully formed, she begins to weep uncontrollably then engulfs every part of herself around me whilst those supple lips kiss my entire face. It feels incredible to have human contact like this after so long and I don't stop her, but equally not reciprocating, for it would feel like taking advantage without truly knowing what was happening. I desperately want to remember, so the affection can never end, but it soon does.

Maybe noticing my lack of enthusiasm, Aria (as I now know her to be - 'the artist formally known as') slowly pulls away to study my reaction and I know she is hoping to see a glimmer of familiarity, but it never comes.

She wipes the streaks of tears from her face and takes a deep breath before speaking rather formally, considering the intimacy we just shared.

"That's OK, this is a good sign. And yes."

Validation that this woman is my wife, to love and to hold until death us do part, and yet I cannot remember a single thing about her. The remorse of this tragic irony ceases all ability to rationalise words or thought and I can only gawp at the revelation.

Leaning down to my eye level, she places a firm hand on my shoulder and utters.

"It's fine. You take all the time you need. I'm here whenever you're ready."

She clearly knows me better than I know myself and leaves me alone with my thoughts. At any other given time, this would be the ideal method to deal with this situation, except at this very moment in time, not a single thought comes to mind.

I cannot be certain at what time I finally moved from that position. All I know is that by the time I felt ready, it was dark outside, the night had grown cold and so I started to light a fire in the living room - a skill I clearly remember learning on that fishing trip with my dad, but now cannot tell whether this is a memory or my mind's creation. Today's events rear their ugly head and unhinge any perception of my once credulous reality, but as I sit and watch the fireplace dance in the darkness, it comforts me to think that beauty can come from such chaos. No two flames ever quite flicker the same and likely never will again, as we too are born into the darkness bringing our own light, which will eventually fade before another flickering light takes our place. We are but a fleeting moment of infinite time, as are all of our thoughts, and the thoughts of those that have been and ever will be. This revere helps in the acceptance that I can do nothing but let time fulfil its duty as a healer, and live in hope that one day this may all just work out.

Amid my philosophic discovery of elementary proportions, Aria's head appears around the corner and I can see that sweet smile beaming through the darkness.

"Mind if I take a seat?" she asks and I nod, shuffling over to make space on the sofa. Lowering herself into the cushion, wisps of dust twinkle in the firelight and a comfortable silence ensues as we become one in a shared moment - no concerns of what unfolded today and what may further unravel tomorrow. Just total calm.

Until I decide to ignite the beginnings of a storm.

"I think I'm ready," I whisper unintentionally before continuing, "ready to hear everything."

She gently places her hand atop mine, looks deep into my eyes and I feel her gaze begin to study me. Her eyes dart back and forth as though reading the scruples I'm unintentionally projecting, before finally offering her acceptance and taking a deep breath.

"Everything I've told you is true, in a way. I was hoping your memories would come back on their own, but it seems your mind isn't quite ready yet for the full unabridged story. But it will come, I promise."

The words strike with a daunting realisation that I may be *ready*, but am I *prepared* for what Aria is about to reveal? Is that what she was searching my eyes for, to find a level of willingness to accept her truth? Well, if she deems me ready, then who am I to argue.

"But how, why, would I forget something like this?" I question.

"Well, from everything I've seen, I think you may be suffering from something called 'Dissociative Fugue'. It's a form of memory loss that your mind imposes on itself as a defence mechanism to protect you from recalling disturbing or painful events. I think your mind has had a great deal of trauma and decided that, in order to protect itself, it must do everything in its power to make you forget - and has even gone as far as creating an alternate reality where you can escape and keep hold of Nia."

And there it is. My clinical diagnosis.

I almost hear it in the third-person, as though she were explaining the bad news to someone else, and I feel the need to retract for some time, to fully comprehend the explanation and digest it as my own. It most definitely sounds correct, and even if I did want a second opinion, who am I going to call?

A sadness soon emanates and it's not due to the understanding that my mind is lost. It's a sadness that comes with the realisation that Nia is most definitely gone.

With hindsight, I begin to reminisce on the dreamlike effects of existing within that other reality, and having returned, I now come to the realisation that *this* is real - unbearably so - and the fact of the matter is, I have to now try and rehabilitate myself back into this reality. A reality that I don't recognise and doesn't seem to recognise me.

"What were we like? As a couple?" I ask, but her reaction isn't the one I've anticipated and the discomfort in her reply makes me feel terrible for asking.

"I'm afraid it's not my place to say. My memories are *my* interpretation of events, and it would be dangerous of me to try and fill the gaps in your memory with my own, for fear of implanting something that your mind doesn't deem as true. A 'false memory', as such. But deep, deep inside there," she points to my temple, "is all the truth you need, we just have to work at bringing it to the surface. And I'm sure we will."

Her confidence provides me with such hope that I feel lucky to have an incredible, well, wife.

"So you did all of this, for me?" I enquire and her blushing face is evident even through the warm glow of the fire.

"I watched you, slowly turn from this great man into a lost soul and there was nothing I could do to help, until one day, you just sat there, and continued to sit there. You were truly lost inside of yourself. There was only so much I could take, and so I packed everything we owned and I bought you here, to help get you away from everything, to make a fresh start and begin the healing process."

Everything she's done and is doing, I can't even begin to understand how much one person could love another in order to do this. It makes me feel awful.

"I'm so sorry I can't remember."

"Please don't fret, it will all come back with time. But now it seems healing isn't our only goal. We need to keep you here, in *this* reality and stop you sinking into the other world your mind has orchestrated."

"How?"

"Well, that's for me to worry about. I think hypnotherapy is off the agenda for the foreseeable future though, I know that much! Almost lost you there."

She laughs and I'm glad the elephant in the room (one of them at least) has been addressed. The way in which today developed was quite honestly terrifying and I would fear ever initiating something like that again, for I also felt the possibility of not being able to return. It was only once I returned and saw her, *this* version of her, that I felt entirely safe - but I don't know whether now is the right time to confess it. Either way, it's all becoming far too serious and so I decide to make an attempt at switching the tone.

"Why do our minds traumatise us like this, instead of just figuring out next week's lottery numbers?"

It's weak, I know, but it still manages to gain Aria's approval enough for a feint laugh, and in all honesty, that's all I'm starting to care about.

9

Today is a day of firsts, I think to myself, all the while sitting crossed-legged attempting to meditate whilst the midday sun glares so brightly that I can see its glow through my closed eyes. The two of us are calmly positioned on colourful foam mats situated in the centre of the snug room, which is quickly becoming the therapy room, although in its current state with furniture sporadically pushed into every recess, one could mistaken it for a home decorating exercise. I hear Aria's soothing voice echoing through the room as I struggle to keep my eyes closed and concentrate on 'clearing my mind'.

"Feel the energy as your breath ignites from the centre of your body, and slowly rises up your chest to become free as you finally exhale."

She pauses for what feels like a longer-than-usual period of time and now I'm unsure as to whether this ordeal is over and I'm currently sat here with my eyes closed looking rather foolish, or whether we are to remain in this meditative pose. The pause continues and I decide to find out the answer for myself. I slowly open one eye and to my surprise Aria is still sat perfectly still with her eyes closed and so I quickly do the same.

"Place any feelings of worry, anger, fear into the core of your stomach and attach those feelings to the energy that is now rising through your body. As you exhale, feel all of those thoughts evaporate into the air as you release that energy." We both exhale.

But soon after, that pesky pause wreaks its havoc once again. I've released all the breath I can - this time it must be over, surely? I slowly open both eyes but once again she remains perfectly poised.

"Your eyes are open aren't they?" she asks with closed eyes.

How did she know? In a slight panic I respond, "Oh no sorry, keep going, I've closed them now, look!"

I squeeze my eyes tightly and straighten my back but soon hear Aria's shuffles and so I look up to find her towering over me with authoritative hands on hips.

"Dion, meditation isn't about closing your eyes, it's about being in total control of yourself, mind, body and soul," she utters, followed by a piercing stare, "that is, if you believe in the soul," she hesitates before ending with the question, "do you?"

It's such a poignant question that it catches me unaware and I begin to ponder as to whether I do, or do not, believe in the soul. I've always loved the notion of every individual having a soul that makes them individual - but soon the Darwinian in me offers a courteous reminder that the brain is a concoction of sensory, motor and inter neurons, all communicating to give the illusion of self-awareness - which finally leads me to understand that I have one simple opinion on the matter.

I shrug.

Laughing, she asks "What *do* you remember about yourself?"

"You're going to have to be a little more specific," I respond, and her questioning quickly turns into a rapid fire quiz.

"Where were you born?"

"Carshalton."

"When were you born?"

"Ninth of October nineteen-eighty-seven."

"Mother's maiden name?"

The questioning seems absurd and I soon put an end to it.

"Are you trying to log me in or something?" I jest, and she laughs.

"I just find your memory extraordinary. You can recall all of theses details - they were all correct by the way."

"Thank you."

"And yet, from the moment of trauma, your mind has just," she pauses, and having spent all this time together I've come to notice something in Aria's idiolect - she takes subtle gaps between sentences, and in that auditory blink I can see her mind racing to calculate the correct words to say next. I assume it's something that comes with her line of work to ensure she constantly articulates her thoughts in the most coherent and polite way to not upset her patients, and I find it fascinating. However, on this occasion I believe it's the first time I've witnessed her unable to find the right words, which both intrigues and alarms me - am I the proverbial Irishman to her Freudian psychoanalysis? I don't dwell on the thought for very long before she finally brings her hands together and then parts them as a sign of 'breaking', then continues.

"And pardon me for prying, please don't answer if you do not want to, but as far as you're aware - Nia survived?"

It's a kind gesture in giving me the opportunity to reject the notion, however I am starting to understand her train of thought on the matter, so I oblige.

"As far as I'm aware, *this* could be the false reality and *you're* just some projection of my imagination."

As much as I meant this in jest, she laughs and I immediately reject her implication, suddenly feeling an overbearing desire to redefine my point.

"I'm serious!" I wail.

"No, I'm sure you are! And who's to say you're wrong eh?"

"You!"

There is some truth there but she takes it in the spirit I indented and we both erupt in laughter at this rather impossible situation.

The laughter soon extinguishes and the image of Nia begins fighting its way to the forefront of my memory. Her joyful smile, her infectious laugh, her incredible wit - all taken for granted. And it dawns on me.

"I'm starting to understand that this other reality isn't real, and I know it's not healthy for me to even be thinking about it, but if there was a place, where you could spend time with someone you love, that's passed, wouldn't you want to be there too?"

"Yes." she answers without a single hesitation and the lack of debate catches me unaware.

I hesitate, trying to explain my next words. "I think that's part of my struggle with all this. If that place exists inside my mind, and Nia is there, and none of this tragedy ever happened, then why would I want to stay here?"

Just as quickly as she agreed, she begins to counter.

"I'm afraid, because you have to live here, in reality, and face your problems. I appreciate what you're feeling, I really do, but it reeks of 'ignorance is bliss'. Your body is mere mechanics without the mind, and your body is *here*, in *this* world. And if your mind is not connected with your body, living in a *real* world with *real* people, then what would you be?"

"Happy."

Dread fills me the instant it leaves my mouth, and I can only watch as her pride crumbles before me. "I'm sorry, I didn't,"

She interjects before I can finish the apology. "It's fine."

Her head tilts slightly and I see that glimmer of hope vanish. I move forward, unsure exactly what I plan to do, console I suppose, but it's too late and she rises to her feet.

"I think that's enough meditation for one day."

And with that said, she leaves the room.

I wince at the thought of hurting her and decide I can't leave it on that note. I hurriedly stand and walk into the hallway, but upon turning the corner I pause and back away slightly, hiding behind the door.

There I find her, leaning against a wall at the far end of the hallway facing away from me, her hurtful sobs clarifying what I had feared most. Making the assumption that I am most likely the last person she wants to talk to right now, I return to the snug room and slump onto the ground.

Everything is such a mess and I have no idea how to fix it. I have feared so many things over the course of my life, but losing my mind was never one of them. And yet, it feels the most obvious choice to fear, for without the mind, would we have the consciousness to fear anything to begin with?

I decide to leave the question hanging rhetorically and instead think more proactively. Aria is here trying to help me regain some sense of normality and I can't even do the decent thing and at least *try* to undertake her treatment with a little humility. It's debilitating to witness the pain I am causing her, and instead, I must do more to help. I may not remember much, or anything for that matter, but her sacrifice to save me means I owe everything to her kind nature.

I begin to close my eyes and reset my posture into a relaxed, meditative pose and restart. Imagining the words she would gently speak, I soon feel my breath creating a wave as my chest calmly rises and falls. However, after ten more deep inhales and exhales, I soon realise that it is not only my chest that I am aware of, but all of my thoughts and the entire space surrounding me. I soon forfeit and open my eyes.

I don't know how anyone can find this relaxing.

10

This-morning's clear blue skies have bought with them a new affirmed attitude, and after yesterday's awful blunder I have decided to treat Aria in the only way (I think) I know how - by cooking breakfast. I've always considered myself something of an early-riser, however each and every morning I enter the kitchen to the smell of toast, eggs and coffee as Aria somehow successfully triumphs in the race she is unknowingly competing. Today however, having risen with the sun, I am provided with the opportunity to attempt a reconciliation for my behaviour yesterday.

After some time, and an array of open cupboard doors, I manage to find all of the basic ingredients to make pancakes - well, all with the omission of baking powder, which is rather annoying since it's not the thin crêpe kind I'm looking to make, no, it's the fluffy American kind, just how Nia likes them.

Used to like.

Whilst mixing a bowl of flour, milk and eggs, I boil the kettle in order to pour the boiling water into the cafetiere and make her coffee just how she likes it, I think - weaker, with a good drowning of milk and a side of her daily newspaper.

I fry up the entire mix, stacking six pancakes on top of one another, then wish the household was a little less stringent on sugary goods, since I now realise this is going to be a terribly dry breakfast without some kind of sweetener to balance the flavour profiles. I do however locate a bag of fresh red apples in the fridge and decide this is going to be my only available option, when suddenly Nia's words, "*Hmm forbidden fruit,*" ring in my ears and I imagine her face smiling at me whilst biting down on that apple with an audacious crunch.

The memory fades as quickly as it appeared and I make the conscious effort to avoid registering it.

I take a single apple, slice it into pieces, then place the segments neatly around the plate's circumference, my bizarre attempt to impress. Just as I meticulously lay the last piece, Aria enters the kitchen, along with the expression I was hoping for.

"What's all this then?" she asks gleefully.

"Take a seat." I command with a smile.

I bring over the plate of (dry) pancakes and place it before her.

"Well I," she begins to utter but I quickly interrupt.

"Wait!"

I bring over the (very) milky coffee and newspaper, setting them beside her pancakes before taking a seat myself - with a coffee that looks like coffee. Her lips begin to protrude and I can see the formation of the word 'thank'.

"No thank you needed. This is *my* thank you, to you. To show you my appreciation. I can't even imagine what this situation must be like for you."

Her smile says everything I need to hear.

"And apparently cooking pancakes seems to be one of the only recipes I know!" she laughs and I continue to nervously ramble, "Nia loved them."

I don't know why I said it, I'm not sure if I should be saying things like this, or even thinking about her, and I wait with bated breath for Aria's response.

"She did." Aria agrees and begins to eat.

Her acknowledgement of Nia comes with both shock and contentment that it's still acceptable to talk about her. Especially considering she's all I can think about anyway, so this will make things much easier and I take the opportunity to elaborate, "I have this memory of her, when she was little."

Aria abruptly stops eating, places her cutlery down then gives me a coaxing nod to continue, I adhere. "I remember holding her as a baby - I couldn't have been that old myself, what, late teens? But I just remember this overwhelming sense of responsibility. In my head I'm so confident, like *'I'm going to take such care over you, no one's ever going to hurt you or love you as much as I do'* and then suddenly she started crying, I guess out of hunger or whatever, but after all those promises, I panicked and immediately gave her back to mum.

"And I think that's always been how my relationship with her felt, making all these promises of caring for her, but always just scapegoating the actual responsibility of it. So, real or not, whenever I see her, I just have this *need* to take care of her. And the more you and I talk, the more I realise why my mind decided to create that other world, not to mask the trauma necessarily, but to finally have the opportunity to care for her."

Total surprise now fills Aria's face, and although I can't see it, I'm sure it's filling my face currently as well, because I've never spoken like that about anyone or anything. It then dawns on me that the woman sat before me is my wife, and is likely aware of this too, hence the surprised reaction. But without the memory of that version of myself, am I really that person any longer - and if my memory never returns, will I ever be him again?

I desist in this train of thought and the sudden awareness that we now both sit in an awkward silence becomes overbearing.

"Really bought the mood down didn't I?" I loath.

"No, that's exactly what you're meant to be doing."

"What bringing the mood down?"

She laughs, "No! Talking about everything."

"It's always so depressing though, how do you do this for a living?"

"Well, not all memories have to be depressing."

The words awaken a sense of understanding I've been taking for granted, and all I can do is gawp in awe of her. A flooding of memories begin to project themselves, each one another example of the times Nia would make me laugh, "She was the funniest kid I ever met."

"That she was." Aria replies smiling and the realisation explodes in my face, of course, she would have known her as well! All this time I'm aimlessly rambling about this girl as though she's a character from a story, and yet Nia would have been her niece.

"Do you remember her?" I immediately question but Aria (or should I say 'Dr Minos' in this very moment, judging by her stare) is giving me a heartfelt yet clinical tilt of the head to say 'you know I can't say anything'.

"Oh, right." I admit defeatedly, "I just feel bad, like I'm always blabbering on?"

"I know tell me about it! It's all about you isn't it." Her humour catches me unaware and a somewhat clandestine laugh finds its way to the tip of my throat.

"Isn't humour against some like, therapist code or something?" I ask through coughs of laughter, and she smiles.

"If you feel the need to talk, then I'm happy to listen," the reassurance feels somewhat insincere until she concludes, "but maybe leave it for the therapy chair instead of interrupting my pancakes, eh?" she jests, which once again causes a rapture of laughter from the pit of my stomach.

And I realise, this is most likely one of the reasons my other-self fell in love with this woman.

The second phase of our day now commences as I lay across our colloquially named 'pretentious chaise longue' whilst Aria (truly Dr Minos now) asks open-ended questions, allowing me to articulate my thoughts in the hope of triggering some sort of memory, when the questions become a littler more specific.

"And how did the discovery of our marriage present itself in your hypnosis?" she must have been sat on that one for weeks, waiting for the opportune moment to slip it into conversation, but I'm happy to explain.

"Well, Nia told me, but you instigated it."

"Me? I'm in this other reality too?"

Throughout the entirety of our sessions, Dr Minos remains a beacon of calm, but my response seems to have truly astounded her, and the subtle lack of focus causes me to falter. I panic at the thought of providing an incorrect response and instead just nod. The room falls quiet and I flicker my eyes sideways to find her mesmerised in thought.

"What did I, she, say exactly?" she asks finally.

I cough up the courage to continue, "Well, when you, she, first arrived at the back door and Nia answered it, she didn't say anything. The two of you just embraced and then I was back here with you."

She remains in deep thought as I explain, and this gap in my explanation seems to have gone on long enough so I continue, "but the next time, when you put me under,"

"Hypnotised." She interrupts, looking to the heavens.

"Erm, yes."

"Two very different things." She quirks.

I turn to her and feel my adolescent self giving her one of those looks. "OK. When you *hypnotised* me."

She smiles approvingly and I explain further.

"You were *still* there. It's like the other reality plays out in chronological order alongside this one. Nia said I go into a dreamlike state and wander around, like sleepwalking, then return, but each time I do, time has passed and I'm just joining back into their timeline. Anyway, so you, she, was upset when I couldn't remember who she was, and eventually Nia told me your, her, name and that we were married."

"And that was it?" she questions reactively.

"Well, then I heard your voice echoing through the house, trying to wake me, then you were just *there*. And that's what it's like, just seamless jumping between these two worlds."

Aria now stares past me and out of the window. I'm not sure exactly what I just did or said, but I'm pretty sure it was wrong. Or at least not what she wanted to hear.

"I sound insane."

This immediately pulls her from the trance, "Dion, no."

"I do! I'm like whatshisface in that film"

"Russel Crowe in A Beautiful Mind." She responds instinctively.

Now, one may hear a penny drop, another may see a lightbulb shine, either way I have something of an epiphany. "Yes! How did you,"

"You love that film."

"I do?" I ask. "I do!" I answer myself.

Slowly, Aria rises a little off her chair and leans cautiously towards me with eyes gleaming of hope, "Did that recall a memory?"

I sit and ponder the question - but with great oxymoronic value, it did, and did not.

"Yes. But not a *memory*, as such, just a feeling of familiarity?" I appreciate I'm splitting hairs here but it's the only way I can articulate the sensation.

I know that film. And I know that, I know that film. But *remember* it? Not exactly. My thoughts feel as disjointed as this film recollection.

Aria's smile soon gleams, "Well that's a good start."

I sit back, sinking into the seat somewhat proud - for what, I'm not entirely sure, but it feels like progress so I shan't dwell on the uncertainty.

"But let's delve a little deeper and see if we can find any memories not starring acclaimed Academy Award winners shall we."

That repartee making me laugh all over again.

Feeling rather bloated from tonight's meal (Cacio e Pepe, for anyone interested) I soon decide it's time for bed, but upon passing the living room, I find Aria sat alone - the fireplace highlighting and fading across her dazzling features. She sips a glass of deep red wine just mesmerised by the fireplace, not even noticing my presence, and I *almost* feel remorse for interrupting, but the overwhelming desire to sit beside her tonight defeats any sense of awkwardness.

"Mind if I come in?" I ask quietly, not wanting to cause any alarm but she smiles and calmly turns to greet me.

"Of course not."

I rather sheepishly shuffle my way toward the sofa as she begins tucking her legs beneath her to make room, and we sit in comfortable silence just watching the fire burn, but it's soon disrupted by uncomfortable thoughts. 'What is she thinking right now, is she thinking how we used to do this together, or is this something new and she's beginning to fear the stranger now sat beside her?' I decide the only way to mask the voices is to use my own.

"Do you worry, that my memory may never come back?"

Without a moment's hesitation she quips "No. I'm a great therapist. Wine?" and leans over, offering the glass. I don't know whether to laugh or be alarmed that I'm currently drinking with my therapist - either way I'm impressed and soon take the glass, sip the opulent berry flavours, then return the glass with a trembling hand.

"But seriously," I push on.

She boldly places the glass down on the table beside her then turns to face me, "I won't lie to you Dion, it is a possibility. It's a very low possibility. But. Yes."

Her brutal honesty doesn't hurt in the way it probably should.

"And how long will you burden yourself with a stranger who can't remember his own wife?" I ask painfully.

Those dark brown eyes stare affectionately, albeit a little glassy, deep into mine. She takes a deep breath then utters, "Well I swore an oath, to bloody God himself, that I would take care of you in sickness and in health *and a lot of other gibberish* but the 'sickness and in health' bit, as a Doctor, is sort of part-and-parcel of the whole hippocratic oath thing, so,"

She lets the final word hang perfectly for comic effect and I actually begin to chuckle like a love-drunk schoolboy.

"Well, each day I'm gaining an extra 24 hours worth of new memories, so maybe it won't matter anyway." As I say the words I know them to be true. What does it matter if I can never remember the man I used to be? Can't we start from the beginning and fall in love all over again? Although only thoughts, Aria seems to answer them by slowly sinking into my shoulder, nestling her head under my chin then speaking softly from deep within my chest.

"This is as much your life as it is mine, just because we were once married doesn't mean you have to give up all hope and live like this if you're unhappy."

I can't bear for her to believe in this notion. After everything she's done and is still doing to save me, just running away is something I could never do again. I gently sit up as she begins to pull her head away until we find one another's gaze and converse with only our eyes. I try to describe what she has come to mean to me, how much I care for her and that the only moments I enjoy being alive are when I'm by her side, but words escape me and we continue to look deep into one another's eyes in silence. I softly trace my fingertips along the side of her face and up into her hair as she brings her hand to meet mine. In that moment I decide the only way I know how to describe what I'm thinking is to show her. I gently bow my head as she pulls herself up and we slowly begin folding into one another. I can feel the feint breeze of her warming breath touching my lips as we're about to meet, but she suddenly pulls away and jumps to her feet, holding her head in her hands.

"I'm so sorry," she pleads.

The fire crackles from the gust of her swift movement and I instantly shrink back into my chair, "No, I'm sorry I shouldn't have."

"It's not your fault, this is wrong, it's totally unethical. I'm trying to help treat you, I must maintain some form of objectivity and keep a professional distance to ensure you get the treatment you deserve."

As far as I'm aware, I've never been a therapist, and therefore cannot tell whether the words she is uttering are true or whether she's letting me down gently - but it hurts like hell either way, and I can only look down in what feels like shame.

The gentle touch of her fingertips soon find their way under my chin as she guides me to look up, and I now see the sincerity in her face. Suddenly it doesn't hurt so much. She concludes, "But thank you," stroking the side of my face as she pulls her hand away and gracefully leaves the room.

I want so badly to run after her and beg her to forget everything, the therapy, who we once were, and start again. But maybe that's not what she wants. Maybe she wants the man she fell in love with to return to her. I begin to envy myself, my past self for ever letting her go. But I quickly remember why I would have let her go, to save what memory I still had of Nia - a memory that is slowly becoming more distant with each passing day. And all at once, my love for them both feels so unrequited. For one can never love again, and the other is in love with the shadow of my former self.

The wine that Aria left behind is still half full and, ever the optimist, I drink every last drop in one tilt of its rim, then take my leave.

I lay in bed, somewhere between drifting off and being wide awake, and begin to stir in my sleep. Trying ever so hard to keep my eyes closed, I suddenly hear the voice of Nia shouting in anguish.

11

Dion's eyes flicker open to see Nia and Aria arguing at the foot of his bed. He immediately tries to stand but his legs remain motionless. There he lay, a wave of paralysis overcoming his entire body - unable to move, talk or even blink, with only the whisper of his thoughts for company, helplessly watching through his peripheries as the two become entangled in a vicious argument.

"Nia, look at him! We need to get him help!" Aria screams across the room whilst packing Dion's belongings into a duffel bag.

"I promise he's done this before, he comes back around, just wait!" Nia begs, whilst following Aria around the room like a lost puppy, glancing at Dion's vague stare as he lay motionless on the bed.

"What if he doesn't Nia, then what?"

"He will, just be patient! Please, please don't take him away from me."

The suffering in his sister's voice is unbearable and he tries with even more might to move or give any sign of consciousness to them, but nothing prevails. As though awakening inside of a nightmare, he begins to logically console himself that this is all inside of his mind. 'None of this is real, any moment now you'll awake back in reality with Aria, and together you'll fix everything.' But what if he doesn't awake? What if they were the last few moments he would ever spend with Aria? Dread now flows through him, beginning to understand that this may be the end of his story, entrapped within his own mind for the remainder of his days, until the mechanical organisms tire, eventually seizing and taking his mind with them. Deciding that is not an option, Dion attempts once again to move any part of his body, but still no sensation comes.

Aria has now stopped packing and in complete disbelief continues to scream, "Is that all this is? How selfish of you! Do you not worry about how this is effecting him? How it's effecting *us*?"

The two stand combatively apart from one another glaring, neither wanting to submit, but Aria is the first to break.

"That's it, I'm going to call an ambulance." And with that said, she pushes her way past Nia and heads out of the room.

Nia pauses and contemplates, taking one last look at her brother laid out helplessly on the bed - her destitute expression providing Dion with the motivation to try moving once again, and with brutal desperation he attempts to signal her. Start small, he thinks to himself, concentrate on just moving your finger. Although unable to stare directly in its direction, from the extremities of his vision he can make out the blurred shape of his right hand, and begins to focus all thoughts onto simply lifting and pointing his index finger. A feint sensation suddenly trickles down his arm, through his hand and onto the fingertip - followed by a subtle twitch. He tries again, excruciatingly engaging every muscle in his finger to just move, and finally it works. His finger spasmodically rises and is poised, ready to inform Nia of his cognitive state - but it's too late and she eventually turns to follow Aria. Crushed with defeat, Dion's finger lowers as Nia rushes out of the room whilst continuing to shout across the landing.

"No! Please! *Mum*!"

Mum? He asks himself, and the word instantly releases him from this mental incarceration - every synapse igniting within his body as Dion sits bolt upright in horror.

12

"Nia!" my cries echo into darkness as the bedroom sits in complete silence until the door swings open and the light glaringly turns on as Aria runs to my side.

"Dion! Are you OK?"

"It was Nia," I pant.

Aria nods with acknowledgement and pulls me in closer, but she's not understanding. I peel the drenched duvet off me and look up at her.

"She called you *mum*?"

The sheer astonishment in Aria's face provides me with the answer I knew to be true, but she says nothing.

"Aria?" I question further - but still stunned silence. Adrenaline gets the better of me and I begin to raise my voice in exasperation for a direct answer, "Aria, she called you *mum*?"

Without saying a word, she simply nods with glassy eyes and I can tell she's holding back an emotional deluge, but the direct answer I desperately need still hangs in the balance. "What?" I ask with disbelief.

Her voice breaks, weakened by the thought, and she can barely get the words out. "She's our daughter."

It's now my turn to enforce the stunned silence. As though carrying a burden too heavy to bear, my mind goes blank, unable to comprehend any one of her three words, let alone in that order.

I finally break the silence, "But, she's my sister?" it's pathetic, but it's all I can get out.

Aria kneels directly before me, eye to eye, like a coach about to explain the game-winning play.

"Think Dion, think very hard, what do you actually remember?" her entire tone has changed, as has her tact. It's Aria's tough love and I despise it.

I've clearly remained quiet for too long and she continues, "I can't figure this out for you, Dion. You have to be the one to remember."

"No, I definitely remember," I reply affirmatively.

"What, exactly? Think as far back as you can."

"I remember holding her. Yes, I was there, when she was born!"

"You were at the birth of your own sister?"

I go to respond but stop myself. Her point holds merit. But no, definitely, it's one of the few things I do remember. Or do I? I have so many memories that are consistently proven wrong, could this be one of them? Could I have masked the true depths of mine and Nia's relationship to protect myself from further pain?

My silence extruding too long once again as Aria continues, "It's not uncommon for older siblings to fulfil the role of parent in family relationships. But is that all this was? A fatherly-figure? Or -" she lets the last word hang, I assume hoping the delay will provide some time for the key to turn and unlock the mysteries of my mind.

It does not. But it does trigger something. Rationality.

I have become my own unreliable narrator who cannot trust their judgment of any situation, be it now, or in the past. The only emblem of dependence I have in my life is now Aria, and if she is wholeheartedly confirming this revelation as the truth then I am left with no alternative than to admit this as my truth also, which ignites a burning hurt. I've never felt a greater disconnect to Aria than I do in this very moment, and an aura of unfamiliarity now divides us as I begin to wonder why she decided not to reveal this to me.

"You lied to me." The words leave me in a soulless mutter.

"No. Dion, no, I've never said anything about," her words tremble in fear as I interrupt.

I tilt my head towards her, glaring. "What else are you hiding from me?"

"Dion, please calm down."

Like reflections in a mirror, our piercing stares refuse to look away, both trying to calculate the other's thoughts.

I decide to initiate first, "I need to see her."

"Dion."

"I need to see her." I repeat firmly then look away into a dark recess of the room.

Instead of distancing herself from my growing animosity, she lovingly opposes the feud and steps closer, consoling me with the single touch of her hand on my shoulder.

"Dion, look at me," I reluctantly oblige, losing myself in those dark eyes, "Nia. She's gone, you can't talk to her."

I shake my head and look away again, "You're wrong, she's still alive." As I say the words, I'm all too aware of their absurdity and can feel Aria's alarming gaze striking the side of my face.

"Where? In your mind?"

I can't explain it, but yes exactly that, and I can only find the strength to nod.

Dropping all pretences Aria becomes enraged, "That's not Nia! That's your projection of her!"

"But she's still there, somewhere. A living memory." I plead, but Aria has grown tired of this conversation and her voice somehow raises without shouting.

"A memory is not real. That place is not real. *This!*" she reaches out and takes a firm hold of my hand, "*here*, with me, *this* is real! Please, Dion, please, I beg of you, stay here, with me, in *reality* and we can work through this together."

I know she's right, but I'm too tired to respond. I solemnly release her grasp and mope towards the door.

She calls from across the room with exasperation, "And how exactly do you plan on seeing her anyway? Your transitioning, it's uncontrollable," I freeze.

Again, as always, she's right. Of course she is, but how can I carry on pretending this is all OK? A wife, *a daughter* - an entire *family* I can't even remember. What use am I if all this has happened and I'm now living as an empty vessel wandering aimlessly with no past to define my present - only a looming future of confusion forevermore. This period of time shared with Aria is the only sense of normality I have, but if I could just see Nia again - having now gained all of the pieces to this chaotic puzzle - would one last encounter complete my fragmented memory? I can only hope, and sometimes living in hope is all one needs to survive.

And within that sliver of hope, I remember something. "*You* can control it."

"What?" Aria questions intrepidly.

"Hypnosis!" the word projects like a bullet from its chamber.

Aria's expression has now changed from exasperation to sheer angst, for she knows exactly what I mean.

"No. Out of the question."

"But it worked!"

"It didn't *work*! I nearly lost you! I'm not risking it again."

Finally reaching the end of her tether, she heads for the door.

"Aria, please!" I beg as she takes a wide birth around me then exits into the hallway. I turn and follow, trying to catch up as she speeds away.

"Aria, please, just stop."

Like pulling up a handbrake, she halts, and without a moment's hesitation spins to confront me, inches from my face.

"No! *You* stop. Everything I've done, everything I've gone through, to try and help you! It's tough love time, Dion. You may not remember me, but I remember you. I remember all of our firsts, and all of our lasts. All of our highs and all of our lows. And I remember our greatest achievement, and as much as it pains a mother to admit it, she's gone, and no version of her inside of your mind is ever going to replace her. I need you here and now, not escaping to that other world whenever this one gets too tough. And I need you to start realising that whatever this other world may be, *it's not real* and you can't use it to solve all of your problems. I'm here, I always have been, and I always will be, to help you through this, to understand and to remember. But I've lost you too many times, and I won't send you back, just to lose you again."

And with that said, she turns and leaves - along with my my discontent.

This solitary time stood dumfounded in the hallway has provided me with a much needed understanding that my lack of empathy towards Aria is becoming far too frequent, and unjustly so. How could I be so callous? She has lost, not only her husband, but also her *(our)* daughter. The comprehension of the latter is still taking its time to settle - but not for her. To think what hell she has been facing.

I soon hear Aria's sobs echoing down the hallway and they grow louder as I near the living room. Before getting a chance to step one foot inside, from the depths of cradling arms wrapped around her foetal position on the sofa, she mutters, "Go away."

"I -"

"Please." she pleads.

I respect her wishes, and go away.

13

Whilst perched on the edge of my bed, I can't help but feel pitiful, over my self pity. Knowing the despair in Aria's voice is something that I have caused - is unforgivable, and all I can do now is remain in a state of self-induced seclusion to allow time for contemplation. Except, I cannot think to even begin contemplating, and so my mind races in a vicious cycle with no beginning nor end.

The resounding word 'daughter' constantly tries to burn itself into my thoughts, but it becomes extinguished with each attempt and soon my eyes focus with a blur as time passes. I can sense the night sky slowly begin to lighten as the sun rises to dawn a new day, bringing absolutely nothing but more woeful sorrow and self-paralysing pity. It's pathetic, I know, but it's all I have, and I want to hold onto it for a little longer before it becomes yet another thing to escape me.

As a listless haze is about to overtake me, the door slowly creaks open and Aria's face appears.

"Come." She gently commands, offering no signal of what is about to unfold.

Without a single word spoken during the entirety of our walk, I keep my head down in shame and can only watch as Aria's feet lead us to the pond situated on the edge of the property grounds. Finally looking up, I realise it's an area of unfamiliarity to me - and right now, looking out onto this vast beauty as the sun beams through the silhouette of trees and warms the water's hue - I cannot fathom why.

Aria sits us on a small wooden jetty overhanging the bank by a meter or so, and here we remain, just watching the rippling reflections of a perfectly pink sunrise - a beautifully romantic setting, were it not for the circumstances.

Eventually she breaks her silence and without turning her head, begins to recite the words I sense she has been up all night rehearsing.

"I cannot think of anything I would want less, than to send you back there. I think hypnosis seems to be a gateway into this other world, which could prove extremely dangerous, but if that's what you want, then here's your chance to tell me why."

She takes a moment's pause then finally turns to look at me, and I begin to lose myself within those deep brown eyes once again, but before turning to stone, I manage to blink and evade her stare, gaining some much needed respite to think of a response.

"You say I don't remember you, but I do. I may not remember the first time we met, or our first kiss, but I remember every moment we've spent together here. And maybe this whole *Dissociative Fugue,*" I pause to let my recount of her diagnosis settle, whilst giving a wry smile - acknowledged through her subtle surprise, providing me with enough fulfilment to continue, "and maybe it is permanent, and you have lost me, the old me, forever. But what if that's not what this is about? Maybe this other world is now a part of me and who I am, because whenever I'm there, something inside of me just keeps pushing me to remember everything, and bringing old memories to the surface of my mind. Memories that right now have no meaning, but over time may start to make sense?

"There must be a reason I've decided to create this other world and hide everything inside there, so why would we want to strip me of that? I just feel if I could speak to Nia, at least one last time, then maybe it'll ignite something in some deep, dark recess of my mind that could answer all my questions?"

Eventually my breath and reason expire. I fall quiet and take another sheepish glance in her direction, just trying to gauge some sense of reaction, but she's giving nothing away. Almost out of panic, I suddenly exclaim, "Anyway, that could all be a load of bollocks, but that's my reason."

After our time together I honestly believed that would get some kind of comical reaction, or even just a smile, but she simply nods to herself - and I begin to realise that I may not know her as well as I thought.

"OK," she shoots, then turns to look at me once again, "as odd as it sounds, I believe you're right, and this other world *is* a part of you, except I think it's more like a parasite, drawing life from within you, and I think you need to make peace with it before we remove it and close the wound for good. Because I'll only agree to this under one stipulation. This has to be goodbye."

I can only blink in response to her honesty and she soon continues, "If you truly believe visiting there will ignite some long lost memory then I'm willing to help. But this is the last time. You cannot rely on some imaginary world to solve all of your problems - and I want you to treat this as a form of closure."

I look out and just stare directly into the rising sun, feeling the warmth of its glare stinging my eyes, but it's a sense of reality I am in desperate need of, and so I wince for a little longer before closing my eyes and making my decision. "Agreed."

Opening my eyes, I see the first break on Aria's face this morning and her smile gleams like the morning sun before wrapping her arms around me. The subtlety of her voice tickles my ear as she whispers, "And one more stipulation. Tell Nia I love her and miss her, everyday."

Her teardrop begins to leave a feint wet trail down my neck as we remain intertwined watching the sunrise.

Potentially about to undertake the last of my visits to this other reality, I sit on the chaise longue and am overcome with a sense of sadness. This may be the final experience I will ever have with Nia and I begin to fret as to whether this is the right decision, or even the right time. But the thought of seeing her again, real or otherwise, extinguishes any feelings of negativity. During the course of this extraordinary period in my life, I have been viewing this ability to transcend into another world as a hindrance, but with this now being my last opportunity to control it, I feel almost superhuman. And whether it's the finality of our adventure together, or whether we may meet again, I cannot allow this chance to slip away, and so I lean my head back, slide my legs atop the chair and take a deep breath, knowing what I must do.

Aria begins shuffling closer beside me on her chair and gives me the look of a headteacher about to recite a set of rules to their student.

"Now, the *second* I see you in distress like before, I'm pulling you out immediately, understood?"

And alike said student being recited the set of rules, I nod in fearful silence. I can see Aria has taken note of my expression and tries to break the tension, slipping into an incredible impression of Bill Paxton, "Are you ready to go back to Titanic?" - it works.

I know that line. I'm not sure how I know that line (or Bill Paxton's name for that matter) but I do, and I laugh. Aria's exasperated shock is evident as she asks, "How can you remember that reference and not your own bloody daughter?"

I smile sweetly and shrug at her quip - not wanting to even begin thinking about the absurd tragedy wrapped in its truth.

She then instructs, "OK. Gently rest your eyes closed," and I abide.

The tiredness from these past twenty-four hours makes closing them easy, but then near impossible to remain awake once they are. I begin to hear Aria's voice fading away in the distance as she recites, "Let yourself relax completely. Just take a deep breath in and exhale, and as you do, just let go and relax."

But soon after, there's an elongated pause, which begins to cause alarm, for I know there's more to this induction - the pause grows longer, louder even, until I finally open my eyes.

14

Dion's eyes open with lethargic momentum and stare into the darkness of intricate beams hanging above him. Reluctantly heaving his aching body from the chair's comfort, he rests on one arm and surveys the room. Neither Aria nor Nia are here. The hypnosis mustn't have worked and instead Aria just let him sleep, he thinks to himself. Deflated, he uses all of the remaining energy to pull himself from the chair and go in search of Aria.

Each exhausting step down the spiralling staircase alerts Dion to his malnourishment, and he cannot recall the last time he ate. Finally reaching the end of his Penrose stairs, Dion instinctively directs himself toward the kitchen, but in passing, notices Aria comfortably laid out in the living room on one of the sofas by the fireplace. All thoughts of nourishment now dissipate, as Dion wants nothing more than to sit by her side. Gently tiptoeing his way towards her, the tranquil beauty in her face grows clearer and he has to stop himself mid-step to prevent waking her. Instead, he silently remains at a distance and simply appreciates her in this moment, finally coming to the realisation that this life together may be everything he needs now and evermore.

"Dion?" a voice delicately asks from behind him.

Dion begins to turn with intrigue, when the familiarity in that voice dawns on him and he hurriedly spins.

There he sees her smiling back at him. Nia. And it's the first time he sees her, truly.

Not wanting to allow himself the escapism without knowing where he is, Dion is overwhelmed by the need to reach for his face - only now realising that his beard has become the main source of differentiation between these realities and, rather disappointedly, he feels the smooth clean-shaven features of his jawline, and so he finally permits himself to fully experience his time with Nia in this other reality.

Could it be, his once perfect family now reunited inside of his mind? The image of Nia standing there as his daughter starts to create a distant feeling of familiarity, but the feeling is fleeting, and the distance grows further from his memory as all sense of here, now, there and then vanishes as Nia simply looks at him. All of him. His true self.

The effervescence in her eyes finally makes him understand - whether his memory of Nia is right or wrong, it matters not, his love for her is all that has ever mattered, and will ever matter.

As though reciprocating his own thoughts, Nia's smile beams even brighter and she hurriedly walks towards him as he opens his arms, waiting for her arrival. An overwhelming rush of adrenaline suddenly heightens then instantly depletes from his body, along with all the angst and preconceptions he had of them reuniting. His legs give way and he kneels before her.

Wrapping her arms tightly around him, Nia rests her head atop his, her flowing dark hair covering his face - and there they remain, intertwined into a single entity as time stands still. The teardrops now trickling down Dion's cheeks begin to hang beneath his chin, until eventually falling to their gracious end, as does this moment.

He looks up to find Aria now standing before them, shaking as she sobs with tears of joy. And for the first time he doesn't see the Aria from this reality, he looks upon *the* version of her that he has come to know and, well, love - he finally admits. This revelation only grows stronger as Nia slowly releases her hold of him, offering permission to submit all of himself to Aria. Knowing these may be the last few seconds they ever experience together, Dion tries desperately to capture a lasting image of Nia - not just her face, but her entire self. He pulls her in close, holding her for the last time, before finally letting go.

Dion stands tall as Aria takes one last step towards him, bringing her hand up to his face and spreading her fingertips to caress every fibre of his hair. Gently placing his hand upon hers, he guides them both closer together, their lips hanging in perfect alignment as they lean towards one another. And whilst floating in that perfect moment, the front door begins to knock.

15

A loud bang from downstairs instantly removes me from the other reality, and I am suspended in animation as Aria remains stood before me poised to embrace in a kiss, as am I.

That bang again, echoing throughout the living room.

The sound gravitates me from the ether and I come crashing back to reality. She was trying to kiss me, *here*, in reality?

"Dion!?" A familiar male voice echos from outside and the change in Aria's expression causes me to abruptly back-away from her.

Terror is not something I've ever seen exude from Aria, but there she stands, trembling. On impulse I turn and head for the front door.

"Dion," I hear Aria warn from behind me, but I falter not, and continue downstairs - her footsteps gathering momentum as the banging continues.

I approach the door in haste but halt as Aria shouts from the stairs "Dion, don't!"

I turn and take one last look at her, that fearful expression still carved on her face, before returning to my stride and heaving open the door.

The sudden blast of sunlight blinds me and I desperately try to define the two silhouettes stood in the doorway. As my vision returns, everything halts to an eerie calmness.

There, stands both my parents. Alive and well.

The shock of seeing them ceases all rationality and I can only muster, "Mum? Dad? But," and before getting a chance to say another word they both flood into the hallway and wrap their arms around me in a rapture of "Dion!" and "My boy!" as I stand in utter bewilderment. I finally begin to articulate something of a sentence.

"But you," the words hang as I pause, the comprehension of what this means is starting to become unbearable, until I finally exclaim, "died?"

Their unanimously resounding "Died!?" is starting to make this feel all too real and as we remain in silence, I see their eyes sharpen in Aria's direction from over my shoulder and I now realise that neither of them had noticed her, and now they have, the entire atmosphere shifts like tectonic plates.

I hear Aria's voice calmly explain, "Dion, listen to me, they're not real, this is all in your mind, please come back inside."

This is instantly refuted as my dad pleads "Son, it's OK, we've been searching a long time for you, just step outside and we can talk through this."

I do not know whether to believe one, none, or all of them. I begin with my parents, "But, how are you," clarity strikes mid sentence - if my *parents* are alive, then - "is Nia with you?" I interrupt myself excitedly.

Ignoring the question, my dad continues his plea, "Just come outside and we can,"

I interject before he can finish, "Is Nia with you!?" I scream.

My parents look at one another inquisitively and I try to gauge their response until eventually, dad, with great patience asks, "My son. Who is Nia?"

Their complete disregard at the mere existence of Nia could confirm Aria's explanation, and in actuality they may just be further figments of my imagination. Oh joy.

I turn to Aria for support, but it's not support that I find. Instead, I find Aria leaping towards me with two enraged eyes and one arm outstretched.

As I flinch, everything stops.

I now stand in the exact same position, instead alone, without a single breeze for company. The rustle of my clothes break the hollow silence as I cautiously turn to purvey the area. Empty.

"Nia? Aria?" I call to no reply.

I take a hold of the bannister and begin to warily climb the stairs, each step screeching throughout the house. Upon finally reaching the top, I am greeted with yet more emptiness. Everything is left exactly the way I remember it mere minutes ago - even the sun continues to burn its midday beam into the centre of the living room. Having now taken some time to try and rationalise this, fear sets in, as the possibility of being trapped within my own mind, inside a sort of limbo reality, soon becomes the most logical explanation, surely? Or even worse, was none of it real? Did I create every event, every person and only now am I finally coming to the realisation of my true-self? My questions are soon interrupted by the knocking of that front door once again. Like a ticking timer about to explode.

The banging grows louder with every step I take and I find myself stood within arm's reach of the front door again, not wanting to reveal what is on the other side. Is this now a choice, could I just stay here, forevermore listening to that tell-tale heartbeat? Or is this an opportunity to finally reveal everything that is happening to me?

My contemplation seems to have a timeframe as the sound grows to a deafening volume, pulsating my ear drums to a point where I no longer have a choice.

I swing open the door to reveal - myself, standing in the doorway staring back at me.

16

Dion stands restlessly in the doorway, dawning a wretched smile, whilst Aria holds open the front door, beaming.

"Come in, come in!" she offers with joy.

Dion nods politely and, hauling his duffel bag over one shoulder, takes a single step into the house as Aria continues, "thanks so much for agreeing to this" whilst extending a hand to hold his.

The tenderness of her touch evokes a pleasant sensation of familiarity, the sort of caress he has missed since their recent separation - something he has promised to try and fix with their planned retreat. Quickly, Aria's grip tightens and she takes one bold step towards him, her other hand outstretched and directly targeted towards his temple.

Dion blinks to find himself now rushing through the grounds outside of the house with Aria following warningly behind him, as he continues to call out "Nia!" - transcending from one reality to the next with dreamlike evanescence.

Although interpreting his current circumstance as though happening here, at this point in time, Dion begins to understand that this has all happened before, yes, the very first conversation he ever shared with Aria after he awoke that night. In the instant of clarity, Dion spins to find Aria once again taking a confident stride toward him, a single hand firmly holding his, whilst her other hand remains outstretched toward his temple.

In a blink, he seamlessly returns to that moment in the hallway and Dion's parents can only watch in horror as Aria continues leaping towards him, taking a hold of his left hand then placing her other atop his temple.

"Sleep," she utters methodically, and proceeds to assert his head down.

And in that fateful moment, I have my first memory.

As though greeting a long lost friend, I can recall a version of myself before all of this, and although mere recall, it's a glimpse of the person I once was. Exact dates and events elude me, but I start to relive an emotion of great sorrow, and as I look up, I see her. The real Aria.

"This isn't the first time is it?" the explanation almost dictating itself through me.

The whites of her eyes glow as sunlight beams through the doorway and she begins to jolt towards me, repeating the motion with her arm outstretched and screaming, "Sleep!" as she try to lay her hand atop my temple, but I retreat backwards and slam myself into the wall behind me, suddenly feeling an object slide down my back. The glass shattering distracts my attention and my eyes look to the ground in search of the sound. That haunting picture of the Victorian woman, once again in pieces, now stares up at me from its final resting place. Even through the shattered glass, hers and Aria's familiarity is uncanny, and I begin to realise this home must belong to *her* family, not mine - yet another lie. As I continue to study the image, a hand creeps over the top and grips the large shard of glass that hasn't quite met its demise. I follow the arm like a trail of breadcrumbs leading me to Aria's terrified face, and before having time to acknowledge the situation, I feel the edge of that glass shard resting against my neck.

"Get back!" Aria screams, the words aimed at my parents, and I finally come to the realisation that she has my right arm firmly gripped behind my back whilst holding the glass shard against my throat, slowly edging its way further into my skin.

My parents do as ordered and slightly raise their hands, clearly unsure as to what to do in this situation, as am I.

"Aria." I try to reason.

"No! Dion, I did this, I did this all for you. For *us*."

"Did *what*?"

A stillness soon fills the air and I'm certain not a single person in this room knows what to do, especially Aria. My dad steadily puts one foot forward, but Aria tightens her grip, pulling the blade slightly deeper and I feel a trickle of blood run its way down my neck. I freeze.

"Aria, please let him go and let's talk this through," he begs, retreating by one step.

"No! Please, please don't take him away from me. I love him."

The stillness resumes as dad hesitates and it's now my turn to take the lead, "What are you," but she quickly resumes.

"We could have been so happy," and I finally hear the tragedy in her voice.

"Aria." I plead.

"I'm sorry. I'm so sorry. I just wanted you to love me."

I cannot see her face, but I can hear the uncertainty in her voice, and I know this ordeal will be over soon. A volatile calmness slowly begins seeping its way into the room and I can feel the release or her grip. Quickly turning and moving closer to my parents, I'm shocked to find that I'm not angry. Her eyes, her face, her entire *self* is just so helpless and she now remains on the opposite side of the hallway with only the glass shard for company, as my parents and I stand tall in unison. Her eyes flash between each of us, like an animal caught in a trap, until her stare finally subdues on me. I can sense her calculating, but exactly what, I cannot tell - and it terrifies me.

Taking a deep, trembling inhale, she finally begins.

"We were just a young couple, it was barely 2 years, but I wanted so much more for us. Then you left me, and I couldn't bear to lose you. I knew that, I alone, wasn't enough for you."

She pauses and a glimmer of memory flashes before my eyes, that's what I saw in the doorway, it was the moment before all of this started.

She continues, "You agreed to meet me here, for a weekend getaway to work on our relationship. And I knew we could have a life together - if only you could truly *experience* it first-hand, then you would believe in the idea of *us*.

"I put you into a prolonged state of deep hypnosis, implanting false memories that would help make you see our potential together."

That's what my mind was trying to warn me, the holding of my hand with hers outstretched, it must be some sort of induction technique - and to think I *willingly* allowed her to hypnotise me.

"Creating a world full of possibility - our happy marriage that was left desolate after the death of a daughter and your parents, so we could start a new life together and rekindle everything that was lost."

So everything I've experienced was her creation, using hypnosis to poison my mind. It is only now that my anger begins to ignite, but I remain silent as she continues.

"But once you awoke, I couldn't understand where I went wrong, your mind rejected the reality I was trying so desperately to make it believe and everything was misconstrued - a daughter you deemed as a sister, and no memory of myself or our relationship. And so I continued to work with you, taking opportune moments to take you into hypnosis and correct the story in your mind - and slowly it began to stick.

"When you called me your wife, I could hardly breathe. And the revelation of Nia being your daughter, it was all I had ever wanted for us. And when you finally wanted to see her, it was only then, that I knew you were starting to believe."

She looks me square in the eye and utters, "But," then raises her hands, signalling to everything around her, by which I assume she's referring to the situation (that she caused) - but my vision is becoming blurred with rage and I try desperately to make sense of what she is saying.

If everything that happened in the other reality was a lie then - one simple question hangs on the tip of my tongue, and I almost don't want to ask it, instead preferring the idea of living the rest of my days in blissful ignorance, but I know I have to face it, "And Nia?"

She shakes her head, and my world falls apart.

"Just a character to help you see what could have been." She confirms with a final strike of the coffin's nail.

So I created Nia, and am now losing her all over again. I wipe away the tear before it appears, but she spotted it. Pretending to care, she gently approaches me and I try to turn away but she pulls my face to look at her as I catch a glimmer of that shard gripped tightly in her hand, and am reminded to fall back into order again.

"I needed you to believe we had a family together. And having believed we lost a child then, with us here alone, we could try again, start anew and have everything we ever wanted!" she utters with far too much vigour.

"Built on a foundation of lies?" I ask with venom, and all she can do is shrug.

As all hope begins to disappear, I guess there's only one question remaining now, "Will my mind ever return?"

"That, I do not know," she answers with false remorse.

I begin caring less and less about the shard in her hand. Stab me, cut me, slice me into little pieces, what does it even matter now? She has taken everything from me, without the decency of even leaving my mind intact. I want to hurt her, so she can suffer the pain I now endure - and as she continues staring at me with those glassy eyes filled with hope, I realise the words I must utter in order to destroy her.

"Leave. Now."

And it works.

Like watching a candle extinguish and become a dense haze of smoke, so do her eyes. But it's not how I imagined it would feel, and I'm soon reminded of our time shared here together. I try to empathise with the woman I just started to fall in love with, but in my moment of woe I suddenly realise she is walking towards me and my heart rate increasing with each step.

"I know there's no future for us, but I just want you to know how much I loved you my darling."

Her eyes never falter from mine whilst I try to stand strong and reciprocate that stare, but cannot help the instinct to look down and locate the glass. I finally catch a glimpse and realise it's hanging by my side as Aria's lips hang gently beside my cheek, whispering, "I just wish things could have worked out differently." And I brace myself, ready for that final plunge.

But it doesn't come from the glass edge, it comes from her lips, and she kisses me goodbye.

I turn and watch in amazement as she passes my parents, stops in front of the doorway, and drops the glass, shattering with finality before leaving my life for good.

Upon hearing the safety of a car engine starting up and driving off, I can finally embrace the parents I had once lost, and now found again.

Their warming touch, their familiar scent, their undefinable sensation of love, all come rushing back and I am overwhelmed with the sense of being a child once again as they hold me with a fortitude that promises everything is going to be alright.

17

I pause and watch as the setting sun forces itself into my bedroom, before returning to packing clothes into a duffel bag. What a moment of self-reflection this could be if only I knew who I was before all of this.

That final glimmer of Aria leaving keeps replaying in my mind, but her face begins to blur with each repetition and I can feel her presence is starting to fade. Whether this saddens me or not, feels too soon to tell, but it's most definitely tragic to think a person could be in such desperation for someone else to love them that they would do such terrible things. The irony being, those terrible things are being inflicted on the person they want to love them the most. The logic doesn't make sense to me, much alike everything else right now, and so I decide to try and stop thinking about her.

I return to packing when my dad knocks the wall and peers his head inside, "You ready to go?"

"Almost."

He smiles, hovering a moment too long, then turns to walk away and I begin to wonder how long these subtle gestures will last - the gentle tones and caring eyes of people trying to help without knowing how.

But something is truly haunting me, "Dad?" I ask.

He stops and abruptly returns as I sit unsure of how to articulate the sorrow I'm feeling, and before my trembling lip can say it all, I speak up, "I miss her so much."

My dad gives a look that I was not expecting, nor have come accustomed to. Reproach? I ask myself.

"Aria?" he asks - his incorrect question answering my own query.

All I can muster is the strength to shake my head. I think her name, but it's unbearable to say it.

"Oh", he offers with remorse.

"I don't even have a picture of her. Just. Memories." And that's when it all comes rushing to the surface. The daughter I had always wanted, now ripped from existence. Except, she never existed, did she? I imagined her, created her. I ignore the urge to rationalise the creation of existence through thought, and instead, just try to remember her and the times we shared - but as I do, I begin to feel rather foolish, as though trying to remember an imaginary childhood friend, and I soon recoil in shame.

As though on-cue, my dad walks over and sits beside me, covering me with a protective arm, "I know son, but I'm sure those memories will begin to fade as time goes by, like so many people that come and go in our lives. That woman has done a lot of damage and there's a long road ahead of us now, but we'll get you back, I promise."

He gives one last squeeze, and it's everything I needed.

I walk through the empty house, pretending to check I've packed everything, knowing full well I have, but secretly want to share my final minutes alone with the place. A house that's been filled with so many lies, but ultimately filled with love, in one form or another, and without having any sense of identity, it has become my only source of new memories - and that's why it's becoming increasingly hard to leave. I feel a part of this old mill now, and whether we enjoyed it or not, we've all shared this culmination of experiences together, creating a binding connection between us and certifying our time and place on the infinite timeline of all existence.

I walk over to the cabinet where I once placed my parents urns and have only just realised they are still there. It causes me to revisit how my life must have acted out whilst under hypnosis - was placing the urns here something I actioned in both realities, or more specifically something that was reenacted on my mind's behalf by Aria? The mention of her name, even to myself, creates a great unease and suddenly the hindrance of hindsight now turns to fear of foresight. In all the commotion I haven't once thought about the repercussion of her escape and what impact that would have on my life now. Where will she go? Will I ever see her again? Am I now destined to remain in a state of constant fear that she will return? Although, with everything having been revealed, I assume her control over me no longer exists, which does provide me with a slight sense of reassurance.

Not wanting to get ahead of myself, I ignore the sentiment and reach out to take a hold of the picture frame situated between the two urns, which contains the photo of my parents. Only now do I realise the power stored within these sheets of glossy paper, holding unique memories that would otherwise be forgotten, and place it safely into my duffel bag. Looking up, I see a dazzling display of dust particles gently descending in the air, as though time stood still throughout the entirety of this ordeal, and has only now restarted.

The sinking realisation that I will now return to a place that I am familiar to, but not familiar with - is likely the reason I procrastinate my leave. Like a captive not wanting to escape, this house has served as the captor to my

Stockholm syndrome, but now objectively rationalising the reality of staying here another minute, strikes more fear than the alternative, and instead I just try to capture a lasting memory, for those who cannot remember the past are condemned to repeat it. I know it's a quote by George Santayana, but I have no comprehension of how I know it - and that helps make my decision easier. I must leave.

This is the beginning of the new me. I will hear stories about my former-self from others, and that's all they may ever be, stories not memories, and I'm perfectly content with that. The events that have happened here will entirely shape the next phase of myself and maybe that's a positive thing, for I know not whether I was once good or bad, kind or cruel, impatient or virtuous, and have now been given a second chance to become the person I choose to be.

Taking a final glance around the living room, I place one hand on the low wooden beam above me, tap it twice and bid the house a pleasant farewell.

18

What has now become my local watering hole seems busier than usual, the grinding of coffee beans, the frothing of milk, even the beeping of that card reader - it all seems so loud today.

Having ordered the usual Americano, I take a seat and open my laptop - yes I am fully aware I have become one of 'them' now, I even find myself dressing the same, sporting a pair of turtleshell glasses for good measure. Since leaving the mill house over six months ago, I have come to the conclusion that when one does not know who they truly are, they will strive to become one of the masses - Exhibit A is yours truly. I thought having no memory of my past-self would provide the opportunity to create a pinnacle version of 'me', but I've found quite the opposite to be true - more a desire to learn how to fit in, as opposed to learning how to be one's true-self.

The glaring white screen reflects across my non-prescription lenses and I tap the brightness down to a more considerable level, scanning the mess of unread emails from agents and publicists wanting to 'tell my story'. How they ever found out about everything is beyond me, but it sure grabbed the nation's attention and, never fully content, they want more. I have started to jot down some ideas and my new therapist (yes, I have a therapist again - remember when everyone was scared to go back into the water after watching 'Jaws'? It was something like that) thinks it would help with the healing process to write it all down anyway, and so I thought, why not heal myself *and* make some income off of my own suffering all at the same time? And that's how I find myself sitting here each morning in this café, just trying to get it all down on paper whilst sipping my first coffee of the day, igniting the senses.

My attention is soon averted as I gaze at the variety of espresso concoctions and begin to ponder whether the majority of people even like the flavour of coffee, or whether they simply need it to be weakened within an inch of its life so that it is bearable enough to drink, so they can keep up with appearances. Or is it because that caffeine-induced high is a momentary escape from reality that the majority of people need so desperately to survive? This then leads me onto having my first memory of Aria since leaving the house. The way she had her coffee, extra milk. Was she too just trying to fit in? Is that what all of her antics were in the pursuit of? A desperate attempt to provide the two of us with a lifestyle deemed by many to be 'perfect'? Could society's high expectations actually be to blame for her wrongdoings? However, that then removes any responsibility on her part for her actions. So perhaps instead, it's the pursuit of belonging, to achieve this 'perfect' lifestyle, that drives people to act out through some innate response in order to survive by any means necessary?

I take another sip, enjoying my caffeine-induced high, and think nothing more on the subject.

As I place the white porcelain cup back down, I can't help but feel as though I'm being watched. With Aria's disappearance, the possibility of her reappearance is something I'm always aware of, and I find checking over my shoulder has just become one of my mannerisms now.

I casually glance up and scan the room with forced nonchalance, when I see a recognisable figure through the crowds and begin to panic. If only everyone would move so I could see properly. I try desperately to look through the blurred rainbow of passing coats, only the occasional break in congestion offering a glimpse of someone, but not enough.

But soon the crowds disperse, and I see her.

Sat at a table on the other side of the room, laughing and talking to a group of friends. I remove my glasses to get a better view then blink in stunned amazement when I realise it's most definitely her. Nia.

I want to call out to her, run over, hold her and never let go, but I can't move, all sensation has gone except for the gentle tingle of a teardrop rolling its way down my cheek. And as I stare, she slowly looks up and catches my line of sight. The bustling room vanishes and it's just the two of us once again, when she beams that incredible smile at me.

Epilogue

The converted sixteenth-century mill house now finds itself empty and alone once again. From a place where time stood still, new life forced its way inside and ignited this sleeping giant, only for it to return to that once bleak, ominous presence. Empty rooms already start to gather dust, windows slowly haze with moisture and those once loved trinkets will now remain frozen in timelessness.

Whilst preparing for the forthcoming years of solitude, those ever-watching floorboards, walls, beams and ceilings begin to reminisce on their most recent residents.

Having taken their first breath in decades, the woman known as Aria entered alone and continued to meticulously leave traces of a life intended for another. Two urns followed by the picture frame of an elderly couple, placed idyllically in the living room for all to see.

Hearing the arrival of their second guest, the walls watched as Aria immediately held out her hand, put him to sleep and then cautiously walked them together through the house, before gently laying him across one of the chairs.

The ceilings would listen each day as Aria recited tragic stories of passed loved ones to the sleeping man she called Dion, who would stagger to his feet and begin reenacting the commands spoken by her, never opening his eyes, before returning to his slumber where Aria would care for him - feeding him when he became hungry, bathing him when he became unclean, and trimming his beard when it became too long.

Then one blissful night the bedroom awoke with a fright as Dion opened his eyes for the first time and screamed at the woman upon not recognising her. The surrounding grounds then watched as he fled to their embrace, where she once again placed her hand atop his head and put him to sleep.

And so it would continue for days to come until, with great intrigue, the entire house watched as an unlikely relationship began to blossom between them both - and their once cold, empty rooms and hallways began to emanate with a warmth they had never experienced before.

But that warmth quickly expired as Dion awoke and bellowed at Aria upon seeing his parents in the doorway. But the doorway itself saw no one, and neither did Aria. She pleaded for Dion to stop, explaining he was imaging their presence - his parents could not be here, for they were deceased. But his confusion and rage erupted and upon smashing a picture of the most recent resident before them, he took a shard of glass and held it to Aria's throat - and in that moment, she confessed.

Pleading for him to understand she meant no harm, and that out of desperation for them to reunite and have a child, she created a single character and implanted her into his mind. Nia.

And finally, lost within the depths of his own mind, the house watched whilst Dion pulled the shard of glass across the throat of Aria, as a flooding of crimson seeped into their floorboards - before packing his bags whilst talking to a presence not there, and leaving the house empty and alone once again.

Now, with only Aria's decaying body for company, the house watches her lifeless white eyes staring into the abyss forevermore.

Printed in Great Britain
by Amazon

19825627R00089